amazing grace

MEGAN SHULL

Hyperion Paperbacks

New York

Printed in the United States of America
First Hyperion Paperbacks edition, 2006
1 3 5 7 9 10 8 6 4 2
Library of Congress Cataloging-in-Publication Data on file.
ISBN 0-7868-5690-4 (tr.)
ISBN 0-7868-5691-2 (pbk.)
Visit www.hyperionteens.com

For Alice Saltonstall
and for
Daniel Ratushny

"So the darkness shall be the light,

and the stillness the dancing."

—T. S. Eliot

part one

three little words.

I am sitting on the floor of the boiler room at the USTA Center. My heart is beating like a hummingbird. My head is overheating, my brain is swirling. I feel like I might puke.

I just puked.

I am not, as my name would indicate, *graceful*.

I wipe my mouth with the back of my hand and dump the contents of the stupid $450 Louis Vuitton handbag that my assistant, Kate, makes me carry onto the cement floor. I find my pink-rhinestone-covered cell phone (Kate's idea) tucked away in the side zipper pocket nestled up next to my secret stash of tampons.

I glance at my watch to check the time in California, snort back the snot dripping from my nose, and dial.

One ring.

Two rings.

Three rings.

Answer, I think.

Four rings.

Please—answer.

And just when I'm about to give up.

I hear her.

My mom.

"Hello?" she says.

I start crying at hello. Strike that. I don't cry. I bawl. It's not pretty. I'm heaving. Moms have that effect, you know, of making you forget you are fifteen and a half, and making you regress to six, clinging to her pant leg at the grocery store.

"Mom," I wail.

"Grace?"

(More sobs.)

"Honey? Are you okay?"

(More sobs.)

"Sweetheart—

"Where's Kate. Put Kate on the phone. Is everything all right?"

"Mom," I try again. "I—" I swallow what I'm about to say.

"Grace, honey, breathe."

I take big, gasping breaths and try to jam the tears back down my throat.

Deep breaths.

Deep yoga breaths.

"Grace? Sweetheart—"

And then I say it. In one blurting crying sobbing mess, I say it. I say it, and for the first time in forever, for the first time in three years, two months, and twenty-seven days. I feel better.

I'm free.

what I say.

You're probably wondering what I say. What I say that will change my life completely, what I say that will take my crazy insane existence and turn it upside down. So I'll tell you. I'll tell you, and let me say right now—besides my mom, you are the only other person who will know. You will know before *Good Morning America*. Before ESPN. Before *Entertainment Tonight*. Before *Inside Edition*. I haven't even told my coach. Or my agent. Or well, anyone.

So here it goes.

I want out.

Grace "Ace" Kincaid, teenage-tennis-sensation-turned–cover girl–spokesmodel, is quitting.

Finito—

I'm done.

five minutes later.

It's only been five minutes since I quit. But I feel like a new woman! The puke smell in the garbage pail doesn't even bother me. My mom is handling everything. *Everything!*

"Grace," she tells me. "Don't move a muscle. I'll handle it."

And if you know my mom, you know she does not mess around. She doesn't try to talk me out of it. She doesn't remind me of the millions of dollars of endorsement deals that are riding on my *not* quitting. She just says, "Okay." To be exact, "Okay, sweetheart—that's all I need to hear."

And it's done.

one minute later.

I am rocking back and forth like a little baby, sitting right there on the floor of the boiler room, clutching my pink, rhinestone phone, smiling the most ridiculously large smile. Freedom. *Freedom!* I can hardly wrap my brain around it. When the phone vibrates, I nearly jump out of my skin.

"Mom?" I answer. *I love my mom.*

"Grace, honey, listen carefully. T is on his way to meet you, and—"

T is my bodyguard.

"T is going to knock on the door and escort you out the side entrance, there's a car waiting. And honey?"

"Yeah?"

My mom's voice is calm and steady. "Everything's going to be okay."

knock knock.

I sling my bag over my shoulder, grab T's hand, and together we race down the maze of basement hallways until we come to the emergency exit. T squeezes my hand. "We're almost there," he says, flashing me a smile. I clutch his fingers tighter.

The wind catches the heavy metal door and it flies open, clashing against the building, startling both of us. Outside, the air is cool and the New York lights shimmer in the distance. I don't exactly know when it got dark, but the sun is down and the moon is peeking out and the autumn air swirls around us. Most incredible of all is that nobody is there.

Not one photographer. Just a big black SUV with dark tinted windows. T opens the door for me, and I vault myself up and into the backseat.

We drive in silence into Manhattan, weaving through the bustling city streets, until the driver turns in to a narrow alley.

"Kitchen entrance," says T. "Ready?"

I take one big breath, stuff my long blond hair under the hood of my sweatshirt, and duck through the side door of the Essex House, my hotel. We weave through a web of underground tunnels, slip into a maintenance elevator, and arrive safely unseen in the presidential suite on the twenty-sixth floor.

I collapse onto the king-size bed.

T stands in the doorway.

"I'll come wake you before the meeting," he says, and shuts the door behind him.

The meeting.

The meeting!

The meeting that everyone else (besides you, me, Big T, my mom, my agent Stan, and my attorney Mariko Chang) will read about tomorrow.

sleep.

The meeting is at midnight. My mom has to catch a flight from L.A. We decided it would be easier than trying to sneak me back to California. My room—I should say my rooms—overlook Central Park. They are crazy beautiful in a totally excessive and over-the-top kind of way. I call room service. For the first time in months my appetite is back. No restricted low-fat diet. I eat like this is my last supper. Sushi. Tons of sushi. Outrageous amounts. And french fries. And cake. Two big pieces of chocolate cake.

I strip off my black sweat suit, run the bath, and turn on the TV over the sink. My face is already plastered across the screen. "ESPN's inside source indicates teen-tennis-sensation-turned-cover-model Ace Kincaid may be pulling out of the US Open. Say it ain't so, Ace!"

I turn it off and slink into the tub.

I close my eyes, plug my nose, and dunk my hair back until my entire head is submerged.

I blow bubbles.

I soak until my skin wrinkles, slip into my favorite pink pj's, and slide into the enormous bed. The sheets are cool and snug. I curl up like a caterpillar and float for the first time in forever to sleep. And I don't just sleep. I dream.

And I don't just dream.

I smile. I'm pretty sure.

In my sleep.

three hours later.

Big T wakes me up with a knock on my door. Big T has been my bodyguard since, well—since creepy guys started leaping out of bushes to take my picture and I started getting weird mail discussing my undergarments. He has a special knock. I know it's him.

I wipe the sleep from the corners of my eyes and grab the plush hotel bathrobe.

"Hey, Grace," says T, from the other side of the door. He's so sweet. Like a big teddy bear. A big, Hawaiian, sumo-wrestling teddy bear. He and my mom are the only ones who actually use my real name anymore.

"Hey, T." I open the door. "Come on in."

"I'm good here," says T, standing guard in the hall. "But your mom's on her way from the airport and she'll be here in twenty minutes."

"Is Mariko here?" Mariko is my brilliant attorney and my mom's best friend. I love Mariko. Everybody does.

"Mariko's with your mom."

"What about Stan?"

"On his way."

T starts to close the door, but pokes his head back in. "Grace?"

"Yeah?"

"You okay?"

"I think so," I say, and shrug my shoulders. I close the door, walk back into the bedroom and, like a giant tree cut down, fall backward onto my bed.

I breathe.

In. Out. I stare up at the ceiling. I have no idea what I have just done. But I hope, really hope, that I did the right thing.

the meeting.

We meet in my room. The five of us. My mom manages to look gorgeous even though it's the middle of the night and she just dropped everything and flew clear across the country to handle my midlife crisis. She's in jeans and a T-shirt, and her long red hair falls around her face. She's beautiful. Really beautiful. I don't, unfortunately, look anything like her. I haven't seen her in three months. I sink into her arms, close my eyes, and inhale.

My mom has this magnetic smile that transcends

crisis. She's the type of woman people notice when she walks in a room. She's just so—

Confident. Like she never has any doubts that everything is going to go just as she has planned. The apple has fallen very far from the tree. I'm a nervous wreck.

"Okay—" she says, her eyes twinkling.

"Okay," I say back, smiling nervously.

"Okay," echoes Mariko, arching her eyebrows.

T's grinning too. Actually, the only one who really looks sad here is Stan. He sits by himself in the velvet chaise lounge, in his crisp Armani suit, looking like his cat just died.

My mom starts.

"We have everything figured out." She smiles at Mariko and proceeds to get the ball rolling on the caper of the century, the master plan. The way Ace Kincaid— teenage superstar—will *disappear*.

the plan.

There's no magic involved. No kidnapping. The Secret Service is not on the case. But there is an elaborate plan—instructions so precise, this whole escape arrangement is more like a *Charlie's Angels* movie than I'd like it to be.

Before my mom reveals the essentials, Stan says his

good-byes. We are officially ending our relationship. It's like a divorce. I have to sign a bunch of papers. So does my mom.

Dozens of papers, one after another, and then, *voilà*—

No more endorsements.

No more press conferences.

No more waking up in strange hotel rooms.

Done.

I can't believe how easy this is.

Stan worked hard for me. Two years ago, we sued the WTA so that I could turn pro at fourteen, not the legislated sixteen. A landmark case. A case that has allowed me (and him) to make a lot of money. More than a lot of money. More money than I will ever need.

Since Stan is my agent, and agents make fifteen percent of everything you make, Stan stands to lose some cash. To his credit, he doesn't try to talk me out of anything.

I'm impressed by his elegance.

"Ace," he says.

"Stan." I smile.

"You're leaving the game on top." He holds up his hand and begins to rattle off my career wins.

"Wimbledon." He raises his index finger.

"The French," he says, making a peace sign.

"Zurich, Berlin, Rome." Stan holds his hand up in the air.

"You've paved the way for—"

"Stan—" I say, embarrassed.

"Ace, Ace, Ace," says Stan, shaking his head and exhaling loudly. (I should mention that Stan is the genius behind dropping the first two letters of my first name. It wasn't just my serve. It was a marketing ploy. "Ace Kincaid, we are going to make you a household name," he liked to say. And he did.)

Stan looks out at the New York skyline. "Ace, you've changed the game. You've raised the bar, you've—"

My mom politely steps in. "Stan, love," she interrupts gently and taps her watch.

"Ace." Stan walks toward me. "It's been an honor." He bends down to hug me. In the five years that I have known Stan Brooks, he has *never* hugged me. Ever. I'm startled at first. But I fall into his arms.

What the heck.

I'm leaving.

No more Stan.

No more Ace.

family.

After Stan says good-bye he leaves. He leaves on good terms and I'm feeling better by the minute. In twenty-four hours Stan will be holding a press conference announcing my retirement. He will call my coach, my staff, Kate—everyone, and break the news.

My mom, Big T, Mariko, and I sit there on the brightly colored couches and smile like teenagers. Except, I am the only teenager. For a second I am overwhelmed with the reality of what I have done. *What is about to happen.*

But before I have time to ask too many questions there is a knock at the door.

It jolts me.

It's like, midnight. Who could be knocking on my door? Nobody else seems nervous. In fact, my mom actually looks more relaxed than ever. She leaves to answer the door.

I hear soft voices and giggling, and I look up to see Julia Roberts standing in front of me. Okay, you're right, it's not Julia Roberts. But she looks just like her. Her hair, her face, she's stunning. As she's standing next to my mom, it occurs to me that they look like sisters. My mom is enjoying the drama. "Grace Kincaid, meet your aunt—"

I raise my eyebrows. "Huh? My what?"

My mom sits down beside me. Julia—whose name, as it turns out is not Julia—remains standing.

"Grace, this is Ava Grady, also known as Agent Grady, FBI, but for as long as you are—"

"Wait," I interrupt. "*FBI?*"

Ava smiles and speaks softly, "Retired."

"I guess that makes two of us," I say under my breath.

My mom clears her throat. "Grace," she starts, "as long as we are going to do this, we have to do it the right way. I want to make sure you are safe. And that's exactly why I've asked Ava to be your escort."

My mom and Ava share a smile.

"Escort?" I cut her off. I thought I was finally through with having someone with me 24/7. I'm almost sixteen. *Sixteen!* I want to do something on my own, you know, without eight billion people making sure I'm "okay."

I don't say any of this, but my mom has this psychic thing going on.

"Grace," she says. "Be reasonable. Look, I want you to do this, believe me, I do, but we have to do it right, and I have to be sure you're safe and—"

I sort of zone out while my mom is talking and steal a glance at Ava. She's younger than my mom. More gangly—with those perfectly defined triceps you get from power yoga. She does not look like your average, straight-faced security detail. She has this—

Spark.

"Grace?"

"Grace," says my mom. "Do you understand?"

Everyone is staring at me, waiting for my reaction.

"Auntie Ava," I say, and extend my hand, "welcome to the family."

red.

Ava reaches into the messenger bag strapped around her neck, pulls out a small brown paper bag, and sets it down on the table.

"Do y'all know how hard it is to find a drugstore in Manhattan?" She dumps the contents onto the table.

One package of hair dye.

One pair of large silver scissors.

"Oh boy," I say, and run my fingers through my hair. "You guys have been watching too many makeover shows!"

"Honey pie." My mom grins mischievously and wipes the hair out of my eyes. "This is going to be a make*under*, not a makeover!"

On cue, Mariko disappears into the bathroom and returns with an armful of products my makeup artist makes me use. She walks over to the garbage can, and in dramatic fashion, drops each item, one by one, into the trash.

"Moisturizing lotion—" *Plunk.* "Extra-exfoliate, good-bye! Bronzer, bronzer? What in the world do you need bronzer for?" Mariko hoots and rolls her eyes. "Toning, tightening, enzyme cleansing! Enzyme cleansing? Give me a break! You're so gorgeous Grace, I can't believe they make you wear this stuff."

It's true. I mean, it's not true that I'm gorgeous. But I'm so tired of having everyone so hung up on how I *look.* Of having to *pretend.* Pretend that every public appearance is the best night of my life. It doesn't matter if you have your period and the worst cramps in the history of the world—you have to be, as my publicist likes to say, *"On!" "Be on, Grace!" "Relate to your fans, Grace!"*

So you smile.

You look like there's no place else you'd rather be.

You can never be real—never actually tell someone what you really think. You start living in this strange parallel universe. And all of sudden, you wake up and you realize that you have no friends your age. You have lived out of a suitcase for two years, and you've gone months without actually hugging someone you love. And even though you can actually afford to buy *anything*, people suddenly want to give you stuff. So much stuff.

Four-thousand-dollar Chanel jackets. Six-hundred-thirty-dollar white canvas jeans! *Jeans!* So you have way too much stuff, no friends, and just—

I grab the scissors and reach for my platinum blond extensions the stylist at the *Teen People* shoot wove into my hair. "No more stupid fake hair!" I say, and with one snip, watch in delight as the gnarly mess falls to the floor.

And maybe it's because it's late, or maybe my spur-of-the-moment snip catches everyone by surprise, but we lose it—

We all do.

I am laughing so hard I practically pee in my pants.

It's cathartic. I'm drooling. My words sound like gasping, soggy snorts. I can barely speak. I grab my hair stylist's favorite aerosol can. "No more stupid hair spray!" I say, lobbing the aluminum bottle straight into the trash.

My mom picks up the pink Louis Vuitton bag. "No more five-hundred-dollar purses!" She dumps the contents onto the desk and plops the pink bag into a large empty box she's marked GIVE AWAY. Then, like a basketball team, my mom, Mariko, Ava, and I pitch every shoe, every over-the-top, overpriced garment I own—even Kate's beloved rhinestone-encrusted cell phone—

Away.

locks of love.

Mariko picks up the scissors. "Grace, you probably didn't know this about me, but I happened to have paid my way through law school by cutting hair."

"What?" I laugh.

The thought of Professor Mariko Chang, Stanford University's most progressive legal mind, cutting hair is—well—*funny*.

"Hey, do you think I'm joking or something?" Mariko stands up, takes off her black suit jacket, and rolls up her sleeves.

Ava lays a white towel on the carpet and moves the chair from the desk on top of the towel, creating a makeshift salon in the middle of the hotel suite.

"Ready?" Mariko says, patting the back of the chair.

I flop into the seat and close my eyes.

I have never had short hair in my life.

I sweep my fingers through my hair one last time.

"Ready." I gulp.

It only takes Mariko a few minutes to cut the remaining extensions out of my hair. What's left is long, blond, and bulky. Picture a big wad of hay.

She brushes it all into one thick ponytail.

"Say good-bye to your hair, Grace." She laughs.

"Good-bye hair!" I say.

She cuts it all off in one fell swoop and dangles the lopped-off mane in front of me.

"I'll donate this to Locks of Love," she says. "To think, some little gal will be running around with Ace Kincaid's hair and not even know it. Ha!"

She plops my dead ponytail into a plastic bag in her briefcase and then continues to snip.

For a few minutes, we all sit in silence—the only sound is the clippers. *Snip. Snip. Snip.*

Enthralled, my mom and Ava watch from the couch.

"Oh my, you look—" My mom sighs.

"Gorgeous," finishes Ava, who I don't really know but I like already.

Mariko hands me a mirror.

Google this: "Buddhist nun."

I have no hair!

I look like some sort of shaved punk-rock star.

It's shocking at first.

I can't stop running my fingers over the top of my head.

Next, Mariko dons latex gloves and smears smelly goop all over what's left of my honey-blond hair.

"The final touch," she says, massaging it in.

I pick up the box of hair dye. "'Heavenly Red,'" I read out loud.

"Heavenly," I repeat, and close my eyes.

ruby.

To complete my look, my mom has a surprise for me.

It's something I've been dying for.

Something I've wanted to do ever since I turned fif-teen.

But I couldn't, out of respect for Stan, who quite frankly, would have had a heart attack.

"You can't look like a freak, Ace." He liked to say. "Mercedes-Benz does not want a spokesmodel with a ring through her nose."

Mariko takes out a sewing kit from her briefcase and removes a small red silk pouch.

My mom is the one who does it.

Besides being the mom of Ace Kincaid—she happens to be a surgeon at the Revlon/UCLA Breast Center. Needles don't scare her.

"Honey, this is only going to hurt for a nanosecond," she says, rubbing some sterilizing solution on my nose.

"Breathe," she instructs. "It will be over before you—"

"Ouch!" I squeal.

"Done," says my mom.

Ava's eyes sparkle. "You look like a Hindu goddess!"

"I do?" I jump up and inspect myself in the bath-room mirror. With my cropped brassy red top, I hardly recognize myself. My mom has put the tiniest little ruby in my nose.

It's lovely.

less is more.

We have a half hour, and I still have to pack.

Except we just got rid of all my clothes! My mom hands me a laundry bag.

"Less is more," she says.

"Less is more," I repeat.

She rubs my newly coiffed head like a Buddha's belly. "*Less* is most certainly more."

Inside the bag is a bunch of my old stuff from home: underwear, a couple of sports bras, my favorite pair of ratty old jeans, a sweatshirt, and three T-shirts. I refold the clothes neatly and slide them into my old backpack. It's pink. It's from seventh grade—the last time I actually went to school. I zip up the pack and sling it over my shoulder.

"Perfect," I say.

My mom grins back at me.

"Grace, honey, before we go on, um—" When she pauses like she's searching for the right words, I know she's about to break some bad news. She did that five years ago, right before she told me my dad had dropped dead of a heart attack. And she's doing it now.

"Grace, sweetheart," she tries again. "You know I can't go with you, right?"

I do know this. I know this in the part of my brain that knows, you know, the truth.

I know that is why Ava is here. I knew it as soon as she walked in the room. But my heart. My heart was hoping that for once, for one time in four years, I could actually live in the same house as my mom, and not in a hotel or an exclusive tennis academy in Florida.

I hug my mom and don't let go for a long, long time.

"Sweetheart," she says, stroking the back of my head. "It's only temporary, we'll give the press time to die down, get you some rest—

"Oh, Grace," she sighs. "You'll get the chance to have a normal existence, a real life." She kisses my forehead and smiles. "Three months, three months and you'll be back home with me."

I breathe and try not to cry.

"Sweetheart." My mom's voice becomes more serious. "I'm laying some ground rules. First, Ava is getting all veto power. As far as I'm concerned, she's the boss—"

"What?" I pull away from her.

"You heard me," she says. "And I expect you to listen to her and respect her. And one more thing. I won't be calling you, and you won't be calling me. It's just too hard." She turns my face toward hers like a little child might to get her mother's attention. "Grace, do you understand?"

"Okay," I murmur with a lump in my throat.

My mom pulls away, places her hands on my shoulders, and studies my face.

"I'm so sorry," she says. "Sorry that I let things go so far. You should never have had to been put in this position to—"

"Mom, it's okay—"

"No. Listen," she interrupts. "Tennis was your dad's thing. And he pushed you. He pushed you into his dream. And when he died, well—

"I think we both hung on a little too long.

"To tennis.

"To anything that would remind us of him. But you know, as crazy as your father was about tennis, as much as he would have loved to see your success, this—" My mom holds up a tabloid magazine with my face—my breasts, really—on the cover. "This is not what your father's wish was, and it most certainly isn't mine. Grace, honey—" She cups her hand against my cheek. "I am so proud of you, and not because of what you can do, but because of who you are. The fact that you had enough guts to get off this crazy train—"

I don't say anything.

I can't, really.

I have dreamed of this conversation so many times, I can't believe I'm actually standing here having it.

And I can't hold them anymore.

The tears.

They are bursting out of my eyes and cascading down my cheeks. It's an all-out flood.

I am waiting for the catch.

Waiting for Stan to walk in and say I'm on some bad reality show.

Waiting for someone to tell me this is all a dream.

Only thing is—it's not. And what really happens is my mom wraps her arms around me.

For real.

one more thing.

I sign one last paper. A paper nobody knows about except me, my mom, and Mariko. And it will stay that way. We agree nobody is to know about what I'm about to do. With the money, I mean. That's just the way it should be.

In the meantime, I will quietly and cleverly disappear. As far as the press knows, I'm in hiding. But as far as you and I know, I will be living, really living—

For the very first time.

departure.

In the elevator on the way down, I smile at my reflection and rub my fingers over my head. "It's so weird!" I whisper to Ava.

"You look awesome," she whispers back.

I can't wipe the smile off my face.

The doorman in the elevator winks and nods politely. For a second I wonder if he recognizes me. But if he does, he doesn't say anything. He doesn't even stare.

Ava and I step out of the elevator and into the busy lobby. For the first time in forever I am not with T. It's part of the plan. Now that I'm incognito I can't very well travel with a 300-lb. bodyguard, now can I?

T, my mom, and Mariko are in a cab, already headed for the airport.

We've said our good-byes.

No press conference.

No media.

No paparazzi.

We walk out of the hotel in broad daylight.

I am free.

flight.

Ava and I take a cab to a private airstrip in Teterboro, New Jersey. The jet, the private jet I lease, is waiting and ready. I sit down in it like I have done a hundred times, but there is a certain satisfaction I get knowing, after today, I will never be flying in it again. We will take it to Seattle and then blend into the crowds and fly coach like everyone else.

Once we settle in above the clouds, Ava pulls out a fancy-looking laptop and starts typing away.

I guess I'm staring.

"E-mail," she says, looking up.

"E-mail—I haven't checked my e-mail in like, a billion years," I sigh. "And Instant Message, I haven't even done that yet! I'm so out of it!"

"A world without e-mail might not be such a bad thing," says Ava.

I gaze out the window.

I fidget in my seat.

I am excited and all, but still, I mean, I can't quite believe what I'm about to do. I stare out the window at the big cotton-ball clouds. I used to love tennis. Really.

I *did*. The game has a rhythm, like a dance. I can't really explain it, but it's the most beautiful thing. *Perfect flow*. You don't even have to think, you just—

You just move. Like a puppet, and God's pulling the strings. But I lost that. That hovering, floating joy of *playing*. Suddenly I woke up and realized I had stopped being Grace and started being this—

I don't know, this *brand name*. Ace Kincaid. Uggh.

And people were counting on me. A lot of them. To sell things—to win. To look a certain way, and sound a certain way, and just be, well, *perfect*. It wasn't like before. Before, when I could just get up and go out and hit a little yellow ball against our garage door. It became crazy. It became not fun. And that was when I knew I was done.

"Grace, honey." Ava startles me out of my haze, she's handing me a pillow. "Why don't you get some sleep."

Normally someone I hardly know, someone I really just met less than twenty-four hours ago, calling me "honey" would bother me. But Ava, she just has this thing about her. You can't help but like her. I wedge the pillow between my head and the window, curl up like a baby, and wish myself to sleep.

four hours later.

"Grace?"

She's shaking me.

Ava.

"We're almost there."

It's already lunch.

A sub, an apple, and a big chocolate-chip cookie have materialized in front of me.

"Thanks," I say, biting into the oversized sandwich.

Ava closes her laptop, reaches into her bag, and pulls out a folder.

"We have to go over some particulars—"

"Particulars?" I talk with my mouth full.

"Yes—" Ava lowers her voice. "Like your name."

"My name?"

"Gotta change it."

"Oh. Right—" I scrunch up my face.

"Not forever, just for the time we're there, you know, to ward off inquiring minds." Ava hands me the folder.

"I took the liberty of giving you some choices."

I open the file and examine the single sheet inside. Three names typed neatly in the middle.

"Pick one," says Ava, making it sound sort of fun.

"Pick my new name?" I ask.

This is weird. Weird and kind of fun.

I read out loud. "Rosamond Brumley?" I raise my eyebrows.

Ava smiles. "Okay, maybe not."

"Kaitlin Kroll," I read.

I like the ring to that. "Kaitlin Kroll. Kaitlin Kroll. Kaitlin Kroll."

Ava scrunches up her face. "You don't look like a Kaitlin."

She's right.

"Number three—" I say. "Emily O'Brien."

"Emily O'Brien," I say again.

"Emily O'Brien," repeats Ava, in a dreamy kind of voice.

"Emily O'Brien." I let it roll off my tongue.

And then, smiling, I reach across the aisle and shake Ava's hand. "Emily O'Brien." I giggle.

"The pleasure," says Ava, "is all mine."

seattle.

I'm not going to pretend to you that this isn't all completely weird. Within twenty-four hours I have totally changed my identity. My hair is gone, my nose is pierced, and when I wash my hands and splash water on my face in a crowded bathroom of the Seattle airport, I have to look twice and wiggle my eyebrows just to prove to myself that I'm actually me.

When I'm done, Ava is waiting outside the restroom. She just smiles and nods for me to follow. Her legs are long and strong, and I work to keep up. Within seconds we blend in to the hundreds of people crowding the walkway, cell phones glued to their ears, strutting along with purpose, heading to somewhere or something.

Ava finally slows down at gate thirty-six, Alaska Airlines.

She glides up to the counter like she's done this a thousand times.

"Hi," she says to the woman behind the counter.

"Hi," says the woman, not bothering to look up. "ID please."

ID! *ID!* I panic. *I don't have any—*

But Ava does not miss a beat. She pulls out her wallet and hands the woman her ID as well as mine. The lady studies my ID and then looks up at my face. She repeats this several times and, for a second, time is suspended—like this is a movie and someone has pressed PAUSE and then PLAY, and all in one motion the lady behind the counter smiles at both of us, hands Ava back the IDs, and punches something into the computer keyboard.

I don't know what trick Ava has played. Or if she played one at all. But it works.

The printer spits out tickets, and the airline lady hands the packet over to Ava.

"All set—" she says, smiling at us both.

"Thank you," replies Ava.

"Ava," I whisper. "How'd you, like, get my picture and—"

"Shhhhh," says Ava, grabbing my arm and turning to walk away.

"Ladies!" the woman calls after us.

My heart stops.

We turn in unison.

The woman cups her hand around her mouth so we can hear over the busy gate—

"Have a wonderful trip!" she shouts.

puddle jumpers.

I've been on three planes in the last seventeen hours. Presently, I am crammed in the back of what Ava refers to as a puddle jumper. Puddle jumpers, as it turns out, are worse than the worst amusement park ride you could ever imagine.

It's not just a small plane.

Not just a tiny plane.

No. It's more like one of those crop dusters—or the plane Snoopy flies, with the scarf and the goggles and the little bubble over the cockpit.

And since you are just getting to know me, I will affirm the fact that I am a complete scaredy-cat, and not the big strong athletic specimen that everyone thinks I am.

The engine starts up, and the copilot—who is so close to me that I could actually reach out and touch him—looks back and gives us the thumbs-up sign.

"Hold on!" Ava shouts.

Hold on.

rock the boat.

After we get off the plane, we have to actually get into a little boat. A BOAT! Where are we going—to the end of the earth? It's windy and freezing, and as the small boat bobs over the dark water, I puke off the side and wonder what in the world I was thinking doing this in the first place.

Ava is speaking to me, but between the rattling engine and my seasickness, I can't make out a word she is saying.

"What?" I shout back.

"ARE YOU OKAY?" Ava repeats, and hands me a

packet of tissues and a bottle of water. "Drink," she shouts. "You're probably dehydrated."

"Probably." I catch a big whiff of foul-smelling fish fumes and swig down the water. And you know, fine, let's stop right here so I can just admit it. You're right, you are absolutely right if you are thinking, Grace, what were you thinking? Why would you leave everything, *everything* for *this*? I'd be lying if I didn't admit that I wish right now that I was anywhere but here. That I wish I could press REWIND and we would be back at the super-swank Essex House, and I could beg my mom to take me back home with her, and I could lock myself in my room and sleep for the next three months. But no matter how hard I wish, no matter how much I doubt what I have already done, I am here, in Medicine Hat, Alaska.

Population 811.

And as the burly seaman with the big white beard and bright yellow rain jacket kindly helps us down off the boat—

Population 813.

part two

"Dwell on the beauty of life.

Watch the stars, and see yourself

running with them."

—Marcus Aurelius

delicious.

I have never been so happy to see land in my life. As soon as I step onto the ground, I want to crouch down and kiss it. But it's dark. It's late. And, well, I don't want Ava to think I'm completely crazy.

And the air.

God.

I can breathe. It's like—

Green.

Green air.

Like Christmas trees mixed with ocean, and when I inhale I feel an ease settling over me that is familiar and sweet.

In the darkness, I follow Ava across the empty

parking lot until she stops at a big rusted-out red truck and throws her bag in the back, which I determine to be my cue to, you know, get in.

Of course Ava drives because, well, I don't have my license. And even if I did, my contacts are all dried out, my head is throbbing, and—advance apologies for the over-share—I have an overwhelmingly sinking feeling that I just got my period.

Lovely.

And the truck?

Picture one of those trucks on *Pimp my Ride* before they fix it all up.

No fancy rims.

No pearly paint job.

There is a sharp springy metal thing jabbing through the passenger seat, and a hole in the floorboard large enough that I can feel the road hurtling beneath me.

By the time we turn onto the main road, it's raining. Not just rain, more like a torrential-downpour-slash-monsoon. I am balled up in my seat, praying that the windshield wipers don't fail and one of those big black bears that you see on the Discovery Channel doesn't leap in front of our moving vehicle, when Ava turns to me. She's smiling. *Obviously driving in a monsoon is part of her secret agent credentials.*

It's weird, but ever since we got here, Ava's kind of more—

Alive.

Lighter, I guess.

"So, listen, *Grace*." Ava shifts gears with one hand and cracks her window open with the other. For a split second she steers with her knees.

Her knees!

"Anyway," she starts again, "I'm going to skip the whole Welcome-to-Medicine-Hat spiel, you know? I mean, God, it's late, we've been up, what—" She looks at her watch. "We've been up for twenty-four hours, so let's save the whole Welcome-to-Alaska deal for tomorrow.

"Cool?" she asks.

"Sure." I nod.

Long pause.

"Um, Ava?"

"Grace?" She smiles.

"Do you, like, smell french fries?"

"Oh." Ava laughs. "I run this truck on veggie oil."

Huh?

"My partner, he was—" She pauses and smiles. "He was really into that kind of thing."

I fold my legs under my butt, pray I'm not bleeding through my jeans, and try to figure out if Ava meant partner, like boyfriend, or partner, like business partner—

"Wait, you mean your boyfriend?" I ask.

Ava shift gears and smiles. "Something like that."

There's a long pause.

Really long.

"Anyway," she finally speaks. "He was, you know, very passionate about protecting the natural ecosystem— cutting down on the use of crude oil, maintaining healthy rivers—" She smiles, and I can tell she must have really loved him, whoever he was.

Ava glances at me. "It's really kind of interesting, historically speaking, diesel engines were invented to be used with vegetable oil, so you don't have to change any of the engine parts. All you have to do is—"

While she talks I don't really listen to the whole eco-conscious-save-the-environment stuff. Mostly I'm still back on her boyfriend, who I imagine to be a bush pilot, or a fisherman, or some other ruggedly handsome out-doorsy type. One look at Ava, you just know that she's the type of girl who has *always* had a boyfriend.

She's just so—

Sure of herself.

As if to prove my point, Ava undoes her ponytail and shakes out her thick red hair like one of those girls in a shampoo commercial. "Oh my lord!" She fans her face. "I am in serious need of a shower." As she talks she rolls down her window and pokes her head into the spitting-wet wind, sweeping her long red hair into a wild dance behind her.

I watch her and wonder where she came from, you know?

She's like an exotic animal, an exquisite bird, a lioness—

How do some people turn out so strong, so brave, so—

Ava reins her head back in.

Her hair is wet, and her cheeks are red and glowing.

"Try it!" She dares me.

And it's weird, because normally, normally I am not the type of girl who does crazy high-risk, illegal activities. I'm more of the seat-belt wearing, rule-following, stressing sort. After two years of professional tennis, I have several advanced degrees in crying, throwing up, and worrying myself to sleep. So, I don't know, maybe it's my new haircut, or the pierced nose, or maybe this Emily O'Brien chick has taken over my body and she's braver than me. Before I know it, I'm rolling down my window, thrusting my head out into the driving rain, and drinking in the air.

This is better than the best spa treatment in Paris. Better than a Swedish massage. It's like—

"Isn't it delicious!" shouts Ava.

The rain is pelting my face.

My eyes are burning.

My cheeks are frozen.

I sink back down into my seat, baptized, and wipe the wetness away from my eyes.

Truly.

I've never met anyone like her.

ten minutes later.

We're stuck.

It's the truck.

"Shoot!" says Ava, under her breath. She revs the engine one more time, but the tires just spit and spin in the mud.

She pounds the steering wheel.

"Sorry, Grace, it's just—" Ava opens the door and jumps down out of the truck. "Stay right here," she says, slamming the door behind her.

Umm, let's review: I am in the middle of the Alaskan bush, it's pitch black out, and I only know one person in a state that is 2.3 times the size of Texas.

Stay right here? Ah, no problem!

I smile to myself and prop my feet on the dashboard. Ava straps on a headlamp, disappears behind the truck, reappears with a shovel, and starts digging.

At first I think she's talking to me, but then I realize she's talking to the *truck*.

"Listen, Little Missy," she says, pitching shovelsful of dirt. "You are not going to quit on me now. I did not travel this far, this long, for you to break down one mile from—"

She digs, and grumbles, and heaves the dirt into the dark woods. I can't help but smile. She's entertaining. And I watch her for a few minutes until it suddenly occurs to me that I should, you know, offer to help, right? I slide over to the driver's seat and jump down out of the truck.

"Can I help?" I ask.

No answer.

Maybe she can't hear me.

"Um, Ava?" I try again.

But it's like I'm not even there.

Whatever. I shrug. I've been up for twenty-four hours, and I have never been this exhausted in my life.

I fish my sweatshirt out of my backpack, slip it on, and lie down on the spongy ground.

Life could be worse, I think, and shut my eyes.

I could be at the US Open playing Venus Williams tomorrow!

I smile.

The air is cold.

Cold and crisp.

A pungent cedar-foresty smell wafts around me.

I open my eyes and stare straight up and—

Wow.

The stars.

I've never seen anything like it.

A gazillion of them, glittering over me—

"Grace?"

Ava is towering above me, headlamp strapped to her head, caked in mud. I can't help but laugh.

"What?" she says, crossing her arms over her chest before finally breaking into a smile.

"Look, Ms. Emily O'Brien, Grace Kincaid," she says, her eyes sparkling. "Whatever the heck your name is." Ava reaches down and pulls me to my feet. "I need your help."

"Sure," I nod. I stand upright, and wipe the dirt from my jeans.

Ava pitches the shovel to the side of the road.

"Slide into the driver's seat," she tells me. "And when I say hit it—"

"But," I interrupt.

"But what?"

"Well, one little problem," I say.

"What's that?"

"Ah." I grin. "I don't know how to drive."

Ava tosses me the keys.

"You do now!"

the cabin.

So we get out. We get out of the mud and make it up the hill to the cabin. And let me stop right here and tell you that if you are picturing a cabin in one of those ski magazines, with a hot tub, a sauna, and ten posh rooms—erase that.

This is a cabin.

A cabin-y cabin.

Think RUSTIC.

Think logs.

Think *Little House on the Prairie.*

It's unlocked.

Ava leans into the heavy wooden door until it creaks open.

"Finally!" she says, flipping on her headlamp.

I step inside and look around.

It's small.

Really small.

The entire space is maybe a little bigger than my bathroom at the Essex House, or a small, yellow school bus. There's a little kitchen, and a sofa, and the walls are lined with books—hundreds of books. I've never seen so many books crammed into one space.

"This is cute," I say, trying to be polite.

"Thanks Grace." Ava smiles.

I walk over to the woodstove.

"So," I say. "Do you like, know them, or something?"

"Know who?"

"Oh, I mean, are they friends of yours?" I ask, dropping my backpack onto the wood floor.

"Are who friends of mine?"

"You know." I look at Ava. "The people whose cabin this is."

"Grace, I thought you knew."

"Knew what?"

"This is my cabin." Ava throws her hands in the air.

"Wait. This is your cabin? You, like—"

"Live here," Ava finishes.

"But I thought you—" I start. But whatever. I'm too tired to even think about what I thought.

Ava tosses me a pillow. "Look, I think we're both exhausted. I can't even think." She hands me a blanket and points to a ladder at the other side of the room. "Your quarters await."

I gather my belongings and head for the loft.

"Oh, and Grace—"

I look back at Ava, unraveling a sleeping bag.

"Yeah?"

"The outhouse is back there." She waves in the

direction of the window. "There's a flashlight on the kitchen counter."

Outhouse?

Whatever.

I'm too tired to even go to the bathroom.

I'll just throw my underwear away. Which is gross, I know but—

"And, Grace?"

"Yeah?"

"Um, if you do have to go to the bathroom, just, you know, talk out loud on the way, you know, sing or something, so you scare off the bears."

"Bears?" I repeat.

"Oh, don't worry," Ava sighs. "Chances are they won't be coming around tonight, there's too many fat salmon down by the river."

Bears! I think, and laugh nervously, because honestly, if I don't laugh—if I don't laugh right now—I'll cry.

I climb up into the loft and fall backward onto the mattress. There is a skylight directly above my head.

I stare up at stars.

Yesterday I was at the US Open and today I'm on the edge of Alaska hoping I don't wake up in the middle of the night and have to pee. That is so weird!

I pull the quilt over my body and exhale a big long full breath.

"Grace?"

"Yeah?"

"Sweet dreams."

"Sweet dreams," I whisper into the darkness.

And I don't take off my muddy filthy smelly clothes.

I just kick off my shoes, listen to them drop with a thud onto the hardwood floor, and close my eyes.

morning.

Sun. Bright warm sun is bathing my face, a fresh patch of drool is under my mouth, and for a good thirty seconds I have absolutely no idea where I am.

None.

When I remember, I pull the quilt up around my face and pretend I don't remember, until I hear Ava. She's talking to someone. I peer over my little perch.

She's dressed in jeans and a long underwear shirt, her hair is wet and freshly combed, and she's laying out strips of bacon on a griddle over the woodstove.

"Great, I can't wait to see him!" she says into the phone.

Who is him? I wonder.

"Oh, and when we come by, you can meet Emily."

At the exact moment she says my name, my new name, Ava's eyes meet mine. She smiles up at me. "Morning!"

she mouths, and holds out her finger as if to say "one minute." "That's right, tenth grade—"

What's right?

"Ah-huh, she'll be here with me." She smiles at me.

"Three months or so. Great, I'm sure she'll like that."

Like what?

"Super," she says. "Thanks, Cal."

Ava hangs up. "Well, good morning!" She beams up at me. "How'd you sleep?"

"Um, fine—" I say. I have that groggy-hoarsey-morning voice going. I yawn and stretch my arms over my head and watch Ava cracking eggs onto the griddle.

"You like eggs, right?"

"Yeah, I do," I say.

Eggs.

I haven't eaten in forever.

My stomach is growling.

I straddle the rail, slide down the ladder, plop onto the couch, and salivate.

Bacon! I can't think of the last time I was allowed to eat bacon!

Ava walks over and crouches in front of me like a baseball catcher. She smells clean.

Like lavender.

For a few seconds neither of us knows quite what to say.

She smiles at me.

I smile at her.

She exhales.

I exhale.

It's like Simon Says without Simon.

Finally, she speaks.

"So," she says.

"So," I repeat, still hoarse.

We both giggle.

"Well, let me welcome you properly to Medicine Hat!"

"Thanks." I nod and smile shyly.

"Grace, I have a feeling—" Ava rises and returns to the stove. "I have a feeling that you—"

She stops, fills my plate with eggs, bacon, and fresh buttered bread.

"What I mean is—" Ava hands me my plate.

"Juice?"

"Sure, yes, thank you." *It looks so good.*

"What I mean is, you're going to love it here."

"I hope so," I say.

Besides the hum of the river out back, we eat in silence.

I shovel it in. My ladylike dining etiquette is apparently back in New York with my fancy clothes.

Whatever. I'm starving!

No nutritionist!

No boring egg whites!

A home-cooked meal!

To be honest, if I were alone, I think I would lift the plate to my mouth and lick it.

ten minutes later.

I'm stark naked, cowering on the edge of Ava's makeshift arctic-freezing NO-HOT-WATER shower, yelping like a wet puppy.

"You okay in there?" yells Ava, outside the door.

"Umm, yeah, it's just—"

"A little colder than you're used to?"

"Ah, yeah," I say. *Freezing is more like it.*

"Oh, I'm so sorry Grace." Ava laughs. "I should have warned you. I guess I'm just so used to it, you know, it's refreshing to me by now."

Refreshing?

Refreshing?

I stand outside the icy spray and strategize how I can possibly rinse the shampoo out of my hair without actually freezing to death.

Oh my God, how can you have no hot water and live in ALASKA!

"Grace?" Ava is still outside the door. "I suppose,

you know, if you're, like, *dying* for a hot shower, I could take you over to the high school. They have—"

"No," I bark. "I mean, no thank you," I say, much more sweetly so Ava won't think I'm a pampered prima donna, which I'm beginning to worry that I am.

"Well then, shower in peace," says Ava.

"Oh, and Grace?"

"Yeah?" I whimper.

"There's a box of clothes up in the loft, some warm stuff, I thought you might need."

"Um, thanks," I say, hugging the tiled wall.

God, Grace, it's only water for goodness' sake.

I grit my teeth and plunge my head under the icy spray until I can't take it anymore.

"That is friggin' cold!" I mutter, and then laugh at the fact that I have started to talk to myself on a regular basis.

I turn off the water, grab the towel I hung on the back of the door, and sink down next to the portable heater.

My hair smells like Ava.

My teeth are chattering.

I stare into the mirror on the back of the door.

God. My hair is red!

It's just so crazy.

"Hi, I'm Emily O'Brien," I say softly, grinning.

"Hi, I'm Emily." I raise my eyebrows and tilt my head. "Nice to meet you!"

"Hi," I try again in a flirty silly voice that I don't recognize as mine. "My name? Oh, Emily," I giggle. "Emily O'Brien."

I say it again and again, like I'm changing the greeting on my voice mail—

I don't stop until it sounds just right.

two minutes later.

Wrapped in a towel, I climb up the ladder to my loft and slip into a fresh pair of underwear and my blue sports bra. I can't even remember the last time I was allowed to pick out what I wanted to wear! No stylist weighing in, nobody painting my face, nobody caking my head with a helmet of hair spray—

I pull out Ava's clothes, one by one, and parade around the loft as the new me.

> 3 gorgeous hand-knit sweaters
> 2 pairs of jeans
> 2 flannel shirts
> 2 boiled-wool sweaters
> 1 down parka with a fur hood
> Mittens

A scarf

1 pair of snow pants—*snow pants!*

Boots.

The boots are hand stitched and lined with fur. They look a little like something Pocahontas might have worn.

My feet slide perfectly into Ava's footprint, which in some weird way is comforting.

Maybe it means I'm supposed to be here.

You know?

Like I fit.

two seconds later.

I settle on jeans, a T-shirt, and one of Ava's cozy flannel shirts, and scoot down my ladder, looking like a lumberjack.

Ava's in the kitchen.

"Well, don't you look comfy!" she says.

"Thanks," I say, twirling like a ballerina.

"Listen, Grace." Ava grabs her keys. "I'm just going to run out and pick up Bear."

"Bear?" I make a face. "Like, to eat?"

"No-o-o, silly!" Ava laughs. "That's my dog's name, Bear!"

"Ohhh," I say, and laugh too.

"Want to come along?"

"Ahh—" I stall, suddenly feeling very shy.

"Oh, come on, it will be fun!"

"Umm, I'm good," I say. "Is that okay?"

"Suit yourself." Ava slips on an extra sweater. "You can read, rest. If you get hungry there's some food in the fridge. Mi casa es su casa!"

Ava pauses by the door.

"You gonna be okay?"

"Yeah, I'll be fine."

"Okay, I'll be back soon." She smiles and closes the door.

But a second later the door swings open and Ava pops her head back in.

"Grace?"

I look up.

"If you get antsy and want to head into town, just take my bike. It's in the shed, okay?"

"Okay," I say.

"Okay." She hesitates. "You're good, then?"

"I'm good," I say.

"Seriously?"

"Seriously." I nod. "Go, really, I'll be fine."

She takes a deep breath and leaves, but it's only a second before she peers back in.

"Grace?"

"Ava?" I giggle.

"Seriously, take my bike! It'll be good for you, you know, fresh air." She smiles this big gleaming smile. "You're going to pass out when you see how beautiful it is here. And if you're worried about getting lost, you know, don't." She draws an oval in the air. "There's only one road and it goes around the entire island. It's like, I don't know, ten miles round-trip, and it's totally safe, really." She grins. "It's a sweet little town."

"Okay, okay, maybe," I lie. I have no intention of going.

"Okay, well, good then." Ava shuts the door, for good this time, and I walk over to the front window and watch her float down the path. She's almost to the truck when she stops, turns, and shouts up the hill—

"Be back by dark!" she hollers, somehow sure I'm going, even though I'm not.

"And DO talk to strangers!"

twenty-seven minutes later.

I'm going.

It's the new me.

This is what I wanted, right?

Freedom!

Independence!

Anonymity!

What am I waiting for? I scurry up to my loft, grab an extra sweatshirt, shove a wad of cash into my pocket, slide back down the ladder, and practically gallop to the shed, where I step over heaps of tools, a tractor, a stack of firewood, a gas tank, and a lawn mower, to get to Ava's bike, a cruiser, with flared-out handlebars, a big fat seat, and those old-style back-pedaling brakes. It's heavy. I lift it awkwardly over my head, retrace my steps through the maze, and set it down with a thud, outside on the muddy driveway.

The bike is red and rusty like Ava's truck, with little flame decals shooting off the top tube. And there's a bell. A silver bell like the kind I had when I was little. I tie my sweatshirt around my waist, then run and push until just the right moment, when I hop on and launch myself down the hill.

three zillion years later.

When I finally make it out of the woods, off the eight billion–mile mud-and-gravel driveway, and onto the edge of the smooth pavement, it's the greatest accomplishment of my redheaded life. And it's beautiful! In the daylight, last night's creepy forest is lush and green and full of birds that chirp and dive in front of my bike like little guardian angels. At the main road, I straddle my bike and look both ways.

"I could go right," I say out loud, and giggle because, well, I'm talking to myself again.

"I could go left!" I shrug.

Either way, I think, smiling. There is not a single person stopping me!

I dig into my pocket and fish out a quarter.

Heads I'll go right. Tails I'll go left.

The quarter hangs in the air, then sinks into the palm of my hand.

"And heads it is!" I say out loud, like a sportscaster doing my own play-by-play. "And here she goes, folks!" I giggle, highly amused by the fact that I have somehow morphed into this bold and daring girl who I'm not quite familiar with.

"Emily O'Brien," I announce dramatically. "Known by no one or nobody! Can she do it? Will she embrace life as a normal teenager and live to tell the tale?"

God. I think I've flipped out.

I sit back on the seat, balancing with my foot brushing the ground, and breathe in.

For the first time in a long time I'm not afraid.

Not even a tiny little bit.

And when I go—

I pedal easily, the sun shining in my face, a cooling

wind on my back. I coast down each hill and barrel up the other side. Before long, I am rewarded with a postcard-worthy panoramic view.

The busy harbor.

The fishing boats.

The village down below.

I am humming along, thinking how great I feel, how sweet this is, how insanely lucky I am—

When I see it.

I see it stroll out right in front of me and—

OHMYGOD.

heaven.

"I'm right here." That's the first thing he says to me. Followed by, "I'm not going anyplace." His hand is warm and strong, and when he slips it around mine, I remember to breathe.

"It's all right," he says softly. "You're going to be okay, just—" He pauses and squeezes my hand. "Don't move."

I have no intention of moving.

I can't.

My legs are wrapped around Ava's bike, a tree branch is wedged in my face, there's mud up my nose, and—

I think I'm dead.

Other than that, I'm fine.

it gets better.

When Mystery Boy lifts the bike off my legs and I roll over onto my back and see his face, well—

He's not cute—

He's gorgeous.

Carved like a sculpture, a warrior. His hair is jet-black and shaved close to his head. And his skin is smooth and tan.

He looks about my age. I think.

And, God—I'm so busy staring at my Knight in Shining Armor that for a second I don't notice that I'm bleeding.

My forehead.

I start to sit up.

"Whoa, Nelly," he says, smiling down at me with this big toothy grin that actually causes my heart to palpitate. He puts his hand behind my head and eases me back, gently, onto the ground. "Hold your horses," he says, smiling this gentle quiet smile. "You battled a moose, and—" He moves close and winks. "I think you won."

Maybe it's the sun, but his eyes—

They're, like.

Liquid.

Liquid eyes.

"A moose?" I say, and smile back.

"Yeah." His eyes widen. "Must have been like, I'd say fifteen thousand pounds or so, and tall—real tall." He holds his hand up in the air as if to show me. "Mating season." He folds a bandanna and lightly presses it to my forehead. "They'll just wander out in front of you when you least expect it."

There's a pause.

I look at him.

"A moose?" I repeat.

"A moose." He grins.

"Like, the kind with the antlers and—" I start.

He nods, smiling.

"Wait, did I like, hit it?" I cringe.

"No." Boy Wonder laughs. "If you had, I don't think we'd be talking right now."

Oh, good, so I'm not dreaming.

So, you're like, real?

I tenderly touch his face, prop myself up, and kiss him, right on his ripe, sweet, lips.

No! Come on. Of course I don't.

What I say is, "Oh."

And I smile.

Not exactly the smoothest move.

But a start.

A start.

three minutes later.

Maybe I like, hit my head or something, because when I finally do sit up, I am talking a blue streak.

"So what's your name?" I blurt out. "And—" I look around. "Where did you come from?"

"Teague," he says, shaking my hand square on and strong, like my mom always says a gentleman should.

"League?" I say, not wanting to let go.

"No." He grins. "Teague, with a T."

"Teague?" I say.

"Teague," he says softly and for the third time. "I was right behind you on my bike." He gestures across the road where a motorcycle rests in the grass in such a way that I can tell he got off it in a hurry.

"What are you?" he says. "Some sort of pro athlete or something—" He pauses just long enough for my heart to sink. I mean, how'd he—

"You—" he starts again, his eyes widening. "You did a full-on three-sixty right over your handlebars. I've never seen a girl—" He shakes his head in disbelief. "And now you're, like—"

"Fine," I say, getting up slowly, supremely mortified that I have become so self-centered, so paranoid, so full of myself, that I actually thought he recognized me.

He gets up too. "So how 'bout you?" he asks.

"Me?"

"Um, yeah." He grins. "Your name?"

"Oh, my name." I smile. "Emily," I say, surprised at how effortlessly it comes out. How easy it is.

"Emily," repeats Teague.

He reaches out and removes a twig from my hair.

I don't even flinch.

And you know, for a second, we just stare at each other.

Right there on the side of the road.

There's this blissful stretched-out pause—

The birds are chirping.

The sun is shining.

It's like the movies.

"So—" he says. "Where you coming from?"

"Oh, um—" I try to remember what Ava told me to say.

"California," I blurt out.

It's clumsy.

"Oh, I meant, where in town—but, you know, that's cool. California, huh—" He nods and smiles brightly. "I was pretty certain you weren't from here."

As he talks, Teague walks over to my bike—Ava's bike—and pulls it out of the ditch.

"Well, Emily from California—" He unscrews a knob and removes the entire back wheel from the bike.

"You've got yourself a flat."

"A flat," I repeat, like I've never heard the word before.

"Do you have a patch kit?" he asks.

"A patch kit?"

"You know, to patch the tire." Teague smiles. *Did I mention his dimples?*

"Oh! Umm, I don't think so," I say. "I mean, it's not my bike. I sort of borrowed it."

God, he's so—

"Okay, well." He shrugs. "Do you like, want a ride into town?" He glances at his motorcycle.

"Do I want a ride into town?" I repeat and point to myself in my second smooth move in one minute.

"Umm, yeah," says Teague. "You, me, my motorcycle, we'll leave the bike here, get you all cleaned up, and come back with the tire patched."

I'm hearing voices—

Three little voices. Inside my head.

Motorcycles are a deathtrap! says my mom.

Say yes! says Ava.

"Sure, why not," says this cute, captivating, charming girl.

The words, they just gush out of my mouth before I realize it—

That girl—

She's me.

five minutes later.

Teague hands me his helmet.

"You'd better wear this," he says, straddling his bike.

I sit on the very back edge of the warm leather seat and strap the helmet on tight. And you know, I try, really I do, to not, like, scrunch up against the back of his sweater.

I swear.

But it's impossible, and I use every muscle in my stomach to not melt onto him.

He turns around.

"You ever ridden one of these?"

I shake my head.

"Okay, well, just, you know—" He takes my hands and wraps them around his waist.

I think I might die.

"Hold on tight," he says. "And lean with me into the turns, don't fight it, okay?"

"Okay," I say, finally letting go, letting my body graze against his.

The engine roars to life.

"Hold on tight," yells Teague.

Um, not a problem, I think, and smile.

"Ready?" he yells.

"Ready," I yell back, but we're already rocketing down the road.

town.

Our first stop, apparently, is for food.

"You'll probably feel better if you eat first," says Teague, opening the door for me, I may add.

The bakery is small and friendly, with light wood floors and two display counters teeming with fresh sweets and breads and every kind of pastry imaginable.

It smells like butter. The real kind.

Butter and sugar with a shot of coffee beans.

The lady behind the counter looks about my mom's age, but heavier. Much heavier. With shiny dark hair and skin like Teague's. Teague greets her warmly and says something in a language I can't understand.

Then he turns to me. "Emily, this is my aunt Sadie."

She reaches out and rests the palm of her hand against my cheek, just like my mom would.

"Look at you," she says.

I follow Teague behind the counter, past the giant

mixing bowls, past the ovens, past the walk-in refrigerator, to a little office with a desk, where Sadie instructs me to sit down in the swivel chair. With Teague watching, Sadie washes out my cut, slathers it with ointment that smells a little like fish guts, and covers it with a butterfly bandage.

"Good as new," she says, and kisses me on my forehead, which normally would creep me out, but there's something about Sadie that makes me feel like I've known her forever.

seven minutes later.

Of course he has a girlfriend.

Of course.

I mean, really, how could I be so stupid to think Hunk Supreme, man of my dreams, could walk through this world alone?

I know it the minute I see her.

The minute she walks in the door.

Her hair is jet-black, like Teague's, and pulled back into two long beautiful braids that frame either side of her face. There's a daisy tucked behind her ear. *A daisy. I cannot compete with a DAISY, people.* And when she struts across the café in her lime-green retro cowgirl shirt and jeans with a thousand colorful patches, all the fishermen stop in midbite and worship, their eyes tracing her path to our table.

Great, I think. My head is suddenly throbbing.

"Hey, Sweets!" she says, beaming at Teague and taking a fleeting suspect glance at me before falling, giggling, into his lap.

She has this feisty-curvy sway thing going on. And as she sinks into Teague's lap, I can't help but notice, well—let's just say her cup runneth over, and if it weren't for the third snap from the top of her shirt—

The dam might break.

Teague blushes, and for a second I want to strangle him.

I'm humiliated.

I sit and smile this pathetically pitiful smile and try very hard to act like I am not completely crushed, like I'm not totally devastated. Like I hadn't already entertained the thought of, say, after we get married, whether I'll use my last name or his—

"Emily," says Teague.

I look up at the two of them and try incredibly hard to summon the same smile I was smiling before Wonder Woman walked in, before the music stopped, before my—

Teague grins. "This is my cousin."

"Your cousin?"

Ahhhhhh—

Breathe.

Smile.

Do not blush.

"My cousin," he says, his eyes bright and reassuring, like he knew just what I was thinking.

Daisy-girl nuzzles her cheek against Teague's.

"Um, hellooo!" she says. "Don't you mean your favorite cousin!"

"My favorite cousin," says Teague.

"Fisher, this is Emily—" He pauses, realizing he doesn't know my last name.

"O'Brien," I say.

"Emily O'Brien," Fisher says. "Pretty name."

This girl, she like—

Glows. And I am suddenly and strangely overcome with a desperate need for her to like me.

I sit up straight and smile my brightest, friendliest smile.

"Thanks," I say. "Nice to meet you."

"Well, howdy do to you too!" She grins, springs out of Teague's lap, strides across the room to the only empty chair, hoists it above her head, and returns with her prize, saddling up to our small table.

"So what are you two nerds up to?" she blurts out. "And what in God's name happened to you?" She glances up at my forehead. "Did you run into a moose or something?"

"Something like that," I say, sharing a smile with Teague.

Fisher helps herself to my raspberry cream-cheese scone, sinking her teeth in and lifting her eyebrows mischievously as she catches my eye.

"So," she says, her mouth full. "What brings you to our little hamlet?"

"What brings me here?" I stall.

"Yeah," says Fisher. "Why would anyone choose to come here voluntarily, that's what I want to know!" She laughs this big hearty laugh that makes the entire café take notice.

"I came to stay with my aunt."

"Your aunt!" Fisher's eyes pop out. "You're, like, actually related to someone in Medicine Hat?"

"Yeah," I lie.

"Well, who!" Fisher practically jumps out of her seat. "Tell us who!" she pleads.

I glance at Teague.

"Um, my aunt is Ava Gra—" I start, but Fisher cuts me off.

"Get. Out!" She hoots so loudly, I'm pretty sure the whole café can hear. "You're AVA GRADY'S niece?"

I think she might choke on the scone.

"Wait." She turns to Teague. "Did you like, know this?"

He shakes his head and smiles.

"Ava Grady is my official bad-ass hero!" she says in complete and utter admiration. "I mean, she's like—" She pauses and shrugs. "I love her!"

I smile at Fisher, oddly thrilled by her approval.

"So, are you like—" She washes the scone down with Teague's hot cocoa. "Are you living with her in that eco-cabin contraption she built up by Eagle Creek?"

Teague rolls his eyes. "Fisher."

"What? I'm just curious!"

"Um, I'm staying with her for the next few months, until—" I pause.

"Until, um—"

I take a deep breath, and I am really honestly quite amazed at how easily it all comes out. "My mom needed some time to do some stuff so I'm staying here until then."

"Nice!" says Fisher. She seems genuinely excited by my existence.

"So you're like, going to school here?"

I nod.

"Sweet!" she says. "What grade?"

I have to think for a second. *It's been a while.*

"Tenth," I answer.

"Same here." Fisher gives me a high five.

"Eleventh," says Teague, who, incidentally, shoots me that same gentle smile that made my heart quiver back on the road.

Fisher leans back in her chair and props her feet up on the bottom of my seat. "So." She smiles. "What's up with your dad?"

"Fish," says Teague. "Chill!"

"No, it's okay," I say. "Um, my dad's—"

There's really no easy way to say this.

"He's, um, dead." I say it and smile, which is weird, because, why am I smiling, right? But any way you say it, it still means the same thing.

"That sucks," says Fisher. Which might sound kind of brash but—

Nobody ever asks.

I shrug and smile a little too hard and try to buy back the light-flowing joy we all shared a minute ago.

Teague stands up. "I hate to break this up, but we should probably get going." He nods toward the window. "It's going to get dark soon."

"Dark?" I say. "It's only four."

"Welcome to Alaska," says Fisher. "Didn't anyone tell you?"

"Tell me what?"

"The daylight," answers Teague. "It's—"

"Fleeting," finishes Fisher. "And it's going to get

even worse and dark and gloomy. Aren't you glad you're here!" With that, Fisher springs out of her seat and throws her arm around my shoulders, and the three of us march outside to the front of the café, where this crazy girl I have only known for forty-five minutes hugs me like she's my best friend.

I don't fight it.

When she finally lets go, she turns to Teague and playfully socks him in the gut.

"Later, skater," she says, and hugs him too.

Sadie appears, her apron still tied around her neck. "You two weren't going to just walk out of here without saying good-bye to me!" she teases, and wraps her arms around Teague, and then me.

"Don't be a stranger," she whispers in my ear.

Then, right in front of me, she turns to Teague.

And, just so you know, stuff like this—

Stuff like this *does not* happen to me.

You might think it does, but I swear.

No.

"Teague." She winks. "This one's a keeper."

home.

I am not a dog person.

I wish I was.

But I'm not. I'm just not. So when Teague cuts the motor at the top of Ava's gravel driveway, and this barking, growling, slobbering, black Lab comes barreling out of the cabin heading straight for me, I cower behind Teague and try not to pee in my pants.

The dog leaps onto Teague, drooling and panting and yelping with joy.

Teague, apparently, is a dog person.

"Look at you," he says, rubbing his nose right up to the dog's face. "Hi sweetheart, hi, yes, yes," he says. "I know, I know, that's a good boy." He pets and rubs and talks that dog language that all dog lovers seem to know. "Yes, I know, baby, I know," he says, scratching behind Bear's ears and neck until the dog grunts and smiles and licks Teague's face.

Yeck! I scrunch my nose and try very hard to beckon my inner dog lover, but *pet the damn thing* is all that comes to mind. Teague likes dogs, and I like Teague.

I reach out and pet Bear timidly. "Hey Bear," I say, faking the doggie-talk thing but missing by a mile.

"Hey girl," I say, embarrassed by the depth I've sunk for love.

Teague laughs. "She's a he," he says, obviously more familiar with Ava's dog than I realized.

Teague crouches down and rubs Bear into blissful submission.

"That-a-boy," he says, scratching his tummy. "That-a-boy," he coos.

Then, you know, it gets kind of weird.

Not, like, weird-weird—

Intense-weird.

Night is falling, a zillion leaves are scraping across the gravel driveway, and the air is suddenly cooler. Much cooler. The two of us sit crouched down right there on the driveway, Bear sprawled out between us, and smile at each other like a couple of sixth graders—

Except I never did this in sixth grade.

The quiet is deliberate, like we're both clutching and storing and wringing out the last bit of this day, and when Teague speaks my heart does this weird dance.

"Um, I feel bad about the bike," says Teague, smiling through the twilight.

"Oh, that's okay," I say, smiling back.

"I'll just go get—" I start, but Teague jumps in.

"I could like, fix it and bring it by tomorrow?" He smiles. "If that's, you know, cool with you?"

Cool with me?

Cool with me?

Um, hello!

"Sure," I say, trying very hard to emit a blasé, casual, under-eager vibe that five years' worth of *Seventeen* magazine has instructed me to do.

But, whatever—I suck at that, and it's only an instant before my casual-whatever-no-big-deal shrug turns into a mile-wide grin.

one minute later.

"Hey y'all!" Ava shouts. She's striding down the hill from the back of the cabin. It's dark, but I can see that she has dirt all over the front of her shirt like she's been gardening.

Teague's face lights up. "Hey, stranger," he says, giving her a big bear hug.

Ava has a look in her eye that I haven't seen before. It's hesitant and careful, and it makes me wonder. "Teague Denali," she says, finally breaking into a smile. "If I had known this is what I had to do to get you to come out here, I would have had Emily visit a long time ago." The two of them share a laugh that is warm and familiar.

"How's the family?" asks Ava.

"Good," answers Teague. "Emily just met a few of them." He laughs nervously. "Hopefully they didn't scare her off."

"Wow, I haven't seen Sadie in—" Ava's voice trails off. "How is she?"

"Great." Teague nods. "Real good."

"The kids?"

What kids?

"They're great," says Teague, getting back onto his bike. "We're all good, you know." He pauses and slips his helmet on. "You should come by. Everyone would love to see you, Ava." He smiles at both of us, flips the visor down, and bullets into the twilight.

one second later.

I follow Ava up the driveway.

She's not talking, so I don't either.

It's like she knows I know something was up with that whole Teague thing, but she also knows I know not to ask.

If that makes any sense.

By the time we get to the front steps she's back to herself.

First she notices my cut.

"What in the world—" she starts, more amused than concerned. "And—" She looks down the driveway. "Oh, boy." She smiles. "Do I even want to know where my bike is?"

I do not need much prodding.

I'm ripe to share.

The moose.

Teague.

The bakery.

All of it.

By the time I'm done, it's pitch black out and the two of us sit rocking in the hammock, huddled under a big wool blanket, basking in moonlight.

"Well, I do declare," says Ava. "The girl is here one day, one day! And she already has a suitor!"

I laugh.

"Yeah, right," I say, even though I'm secretly hoping that it's true.

"Well," says Ava, a certain magic in her voice. "I've known Teague since he was—" She counts on her fingers. "Since he was five years old, and darlin', trust me, that boy is SWEET ON YOU!"

She laughs.

"You think?" I say, smiling. Wanting to hear it again.

"He is a gem," she says. And as she says it, this quiet peaceful look washes over her face. It's kind of sad and sweet all at the same time.

I'm dying to ask Ava how she knows Teague.

How she knows his family.

How they know her—

But something tells me that she doesn't really want to go there, something about the look in her eyes—

Anyway, I'm starved.

"Come on, my little Juliet," she teases, and lunges out of the hammock, making me almost fall out backward.

"Let's eat!"

dinner.

Inside, the cabin is warm and cozy, and the table is already set—covered with a rich red tablecloth and adorned with a vase full of wildflowers. The candles smell like honey, and the bowls are carved of dark soft wood. It's tranquil and lovely, and when I sit down, I feel tranquil and lovely too.

Ava sets the food down and slides into the seat across from me. "Do you want to say grace?" she asks, before realizing her unintentional play on words.

"Grace," she starts again. "Let's say grace." Ava reaches out across the table and lightly covers my hands with hers. And whatever, maybe you think this is weird or corny or strange, but I don't know how to explain it. Everything Ava does seems like the best idea, and I follow her instructions like a devoted little sister.

Ava shuts her eyes. I keep mine open at first, but I feel like I'm cheating so I shut my eyes too.

"Thank you for this beautiful evening—" she says.

"Thank you for bringing Grace—" She squeezes my hand.

"Thank you for this glorious night—" She pauses. "Thank you for good health, for stars, for Bear—"

There's a long moment of silence, and I crack one eye open and peer through the candlelight.

And, you know, maybe I'm overly emotional due to the fact that I have my period and just completely changed my life. But a tear, an itsy bitsy lone tear is welled up in the corner of my eye.

Ava smiles with her eyes closed.

"These," she whispers, "these are fortunate days."

paradise.

I have three servings of mashed potatoes, salad from Ava's garden, and salmon so fresh and buttery I think it might be the best meal I have ever had. After dinner I collapse onto the couch.

"Hey, princess," teases Ava. "How 'bout a little help here?"

"Oh, sorry," I say, jumping up, embarrassed that I didn't offer to help. "I've got it," I say, taking the plates out of Ava's hands.

"How about we do them together," she says, tossing me a dish towel and rolling up her sleeves. "But first, we need to boil the water."

"Boil the water?"

"We don't have hot water, so we have to boil it first."

"Oh, sorry."

"Don't be sorry." Ava slips an apron over her neck. "It's just that—" She reaches above the sink and retrieves a large metal pot. "Everything is just a little harder when you live in paradise."

I help Ava fill the pot, cart it over to the woodstove, where we wait for it to boil, and carry it back to the kitchen, somehow managing to not spill scalding hot water on either of us. She begins her instructions. "First," she tells me. "You have to be super frugal with the water."

She talks as she fills the second sink basin. "All the water in the cabin comes from a spring. It's pretty good water, but you don't want to drink it, it's unfiltered. So for drinking, we use bottled water from town. For bathing and washing, we use the water from the spring."

I nod.

"It's hard to get used to at first," says Ava. "But after a few days, you'll adapt to it all, no problem." Ava bends down and points to the pail under the drain in the sink. "This collects the gray water, that basically is any water that doesn't have poop in it and doesn't need to be treated."

"Ew," I say under my breath.

"Well, hey, that's what it is." She laughs. "No indoor plumbing, toots."

I smile nervously.

"Gray water is water with soap in it or like, food particles, or water from washing clothes. Once I have the system set, the gray water will drain into a deep pit out by the garden, and the ground will absorb it."

I take a big deep breath.

"I know." Ava smiles. "It's a lot. And until I have a better system, which I'm working on, by the way, we need to carry the gray water outside and dump it into a pit out back. The good news is that it's great for the soil, and that way there's no waste." She hands me the sponge. "Have a blast," she says, walking away.

"Um, Ava?"

Ava turns back toward me.

"Do you ever get, like—" I scrunch up my nose. "I don't know, get like, tired of doing all of this?"

"Well, yeah." She smiles. "Washing the dishes can be a royal pain, and sometimes in the dead of winter I have dreams of long hot baths and not having to get up and traipse outside to pee." Ava walks over to the window and looks out at the night sky. "But most of all I love how quiet it is, and how I can step out the door and just sit and listen." She pauses for a really long time. "The winters can be brutal—the terrain, the lack of sunlight—I won't lie, it can be tough." She sighs deeply. "But for me, living out here—" Her face lights up. "This is the only place I really feel—home."

tea.

I haul the gray water out past the garden and dump it into the soil pit, stumble back into the cabin, and collapse onto the couch. Dishes done. Ava sits scrunched up opposite me, a pair of red glasses resting librarian style on the tip of her nose. She is completely absorbed in a book much thicker than anything I have ever read. I tilt my head to read the title, *The A to Z Guide to Composting Toilets*.

I don't seem to be good at initiating conversation, so I make a big production of hauling myself off the couch and traveling across the hardwood floor to the bookshelf, where I sigh and scan for a book I have no intention of reading. I settle on an oversized volume with glossy photos, *The Complete Guide to Building an Eco House*, flop back onto the couch, and flip through the pictures. But no matter what page I look at all I see is Teague. Let's face it, I'm in love, and when you're in love, it is very difficult to read a book. I turn the pages kind of louder than I need to until Ava finally falls prey to my game.

She peers over her glasses. "You okay?" she asks, smiling.

"Um, yeah," I lie. As soon as the words slip out of my mouth I want to kick myself.

Ava returns her nose to her book.

I fidget.

I flop.

I fold and refold my legs under my butt.

"How is your head?" she says, finally closing her book.

"Oh." I reach up and feel the bandage, Sadie's bandage. "Good," I answer. "I mean, it doesn't really hurt unless I touch it."

"Good." Ava takes off her glasses.

"So," she says. "School starts on Monday—nervous?"

"Sort of." I shrug. "And sort of excited, I guess."

"Understandable." Ava rises from the sofa and walks into the kitchen. "Do you want some tea?"

"Sure, thanks."

"Peppermint?"

"Sounds good."

Ava sets the teapot on the woodstove.

"So." She grins. "How was your first day?"

"Pretty good," I say, really wishing I could say what I feel, which is that it wasn't just pretty good, it was the best day of my teenage life.

"Pretty good?" jokes Ava, pouring us both a cup of tea. She hands me mine. "With the exception of almost cracking your head open, seems like you have no problem making friends."

"I guess." I blush again and take a sip. *Too hot.*

"How'd you like Fisher?" she asks.

"She's—" I search for the right word.

"Crazy!" says Ava. "But good crazy, for the most part."

"Yeah." I nod. "She seems really nice."

There's a long pause.

"So," I try to sound casual. "Um, how do you like, know all those guys?"

"Who, Teague?"

"Yeah," I say, it's awkward. "Yeah, I mean, all those guys."

Ava takes a mile-long sigh.

"Long story," she says, smiling kind of bravely, her lips pursed together. "I'll tell you, some time." Ava takes another sip of tea. "Not now, though."

"Okay," I answer, and desperately try to think of something else to say, something that will take the ache off Ava's face.

"Hey," I blurt out. "How am I going to get to school?" I sit up straight, pleased with my adept subject change.

Ava perks up too. "Oh." She laughs. "You might not like me after you know this—"

"Tell me!" I say, and note, oddly, that I sound just like Fisher in the bakery.

"You're going to have to hike down the driveway and catch the bus." She smiles. "All the way down to the main road."

"The bus? A real yellow school bus?"

Ava laughs. "Yes, a real yellow school bus, is there another kind?"

"Well, no, it's just that, well, I've always wanted to ride one of those."

"Really?"

"It's like, I don't know, very ordinary. I crave ordinary."

"Well, don't get too excited." Ava grins. "I think it might lose its luster after week one. When the snow comes, you can ride my Honda."

"Your Honda?"

"Snowmobile," says Ava. "You don't need a license, so you can—"

"I get to drive!"

"Settle down." She laughs. "This is assuming you will always, always, *always* wear a helmet. Do you understand?"

"No problem," I answer, and run my fingers over my cut.

Ava stands up and blows out the candles on the table.

"Listen, I'm beat," she says.

"Me too." I heave myself up off the couch like an old lady, and think about how good it feels to be tired, and fed, and have a warm bed. I think about Teague, and Fisher, and Sadie's fish ointment, and how none of them have any idea who I really am. How, for the first time in a long time I can just be me. Which, to be honest, feels better than I can possibly explain.

alone.

In the morning I skip the arctic shower in favor of my grubby jeans and an old green T-shirt from Ava's collection.

Ava, by the way, is nowhere to be found.

No eggs, no bacon. No hot buttered bread.

I am left to my own devices.

My prior cooking experience consists of watching *Iron Chef* reruns, so you can understand that I am giddy with excitement when I grab the clippers from the cabinet by the sink and forage through the garden. The day is gorgeous and bright, and under a blanket of clear blue sky I gather garlic, some oniony-smelling greens that I hope are chives, basil, and one juicy ripe tomato that's calling my name.

Back in the cabin, I slip on Ava's apron, carefully

remove this giant meat cleaver–looking knife from the wall, and set my bounty on a wooden cutting board that I find under the sink. As I chop the greens into tiny slivers, I wonder why in the world I am fifteen years old and I have never cooked for myself. *It's embarrassing, is what it is!*

I warm up the pan on the woodstove and sauté the greens in butter, whip the eggs in a separate glass measuring bowl, and pour them onto the hot pan. Lucky I've seen my nutritionist do this so many times. If only with egg whites. When it's all said and done, I have quite possibly created the finest omelet in my life. Some might say it looks like a pile of mush. But to me it's beautiful. If an omelet can be beautiful—

This one is.

I top it off with shavings of cheddar cheese, basil, and thin slices of tomato, and just as I pour myself a glass of tea and sit down at the table, Ava breezes in.

"Well, well, well," she says, returning my smile. "Looks like you rustled up some breakfast."

"Looks like it." I laugh. "I took some stuff from the garden, is that okay?"

"Of course!" answers Ava, her hair tied back and her face covered with random streaks of black grease, like she's already taken apart and put together an entire engine.

"I am so glad you helped yourself." She sets down her stuff: a mesh sack filled with groceries, a backpack, and a rolled-up newspaper. "I should have left you a note, but I thought—" She looks at her watch. "Wow, it's ten already! Anyway, I thought I'd be back before you woke up, but I obviously thought wrong."

Ava sits down across from me.

"No worries," I say, taking my first bite.

"So," says Ava. "How'd you sleep?"

"Good," I say. "I mean, well," I correct myself. "I slept well. Do you want some?" I push my plate toward her.

"Oh, no, thank you, though—it looks great."

"It's pretty good." I shrug.

"Well, I stopped by Sadie's and had three blueberry muffins. Those muffins—" Ava exhales like she's full. "Sadie makes the best muffins."

"You stopped by Sadie's?" I say, surprised. *I mean, the way Teague was talking it sounded like—*

"Yes, and—" Ava cocks an eyebrow. "I must say, you, my dear, made quite an impression."

"I did?" I'm shameless. I can't help it. I want to hear it again.

"You are the talk of the town." She grins.

"I am?"

For a second I'm worried, you know, that someone—

"Oh, not like that, silly." Ava winks. "Believe me, nobody in Medicine Hat would recognize you. What I meant was, they loved you! Sadie thought you were sweet—no, wait." Ava pauses. "I think her exact word was *adorable*."

I blush.

"So like, did you see anyone else?" I ask.

Lame. Lame. Lame! I know. But I'm a little too shy to just come out and ask about Teague.

"Hmmm, well, I saw a whole bunch of fishermen. I saw Cory Foster, who will be your teacher. And, oh, I saw—" Ava turns to pet Bear and stops for what seems like an eternity, distracted by Bear's wet nose.

"Um," I stammer. *I'm in suspense here!* "Who'd you see?"

Ava is busy scratching the back of Bear's ears. "Oh, I saw—" Ava nuzzles her nose up to Bear's. "Yes, you like that, don't you—"

"Um, so—" I try hard to sound casual. "Who'd you see?"

"Oh, sorry. I saw Fisher. She thought you were, how did she put it?" Ava laughs. "Cool as shit, I think were her exact words." Ava smiles at me. "Which I think is a compliment?"

I smile.

"Oh, and—" Ava stops again and scratches Bear's

tummy. "Yes, you like that, don't you. Yes, you do—"

"Sorry," she says, finally letting go of Bear. "It's just, this dog is so darn cute!

"Anyway, Fisher said she might come by tonight and take you out on the town."

"Really?" I am thrilled by this news. It's like I'm back in seventh grade and the coolest girl in school just invited me to sit at her table.

"I take it that's cool with you?"

"Definitely."

"Good, because I told her that would be great." Ava gets up and starts unloading the groceries. "Of course, I told her she has to have you back by midnight, which, by the way, is your official curfew, understood?"

"Understood."

"Fisher mentioned something about bowling."

"Bowling?"

"Is that not your thing?"

"No, no, it's cool," I answer. "I just haven't gone, in like, a million years."

"Well, it's time to have a little fun! And you never know—"

"Never know what?" I ask.

Ava wiggles her eyebrows. "Maybe your *boy*friend will be there."

"What*ever*," I say.

But really, I don't mind the teasing.

I don't mind at all.

a little later.

I am in the hammock when Ava informs me it is time to work. "Let's go, Grace," she says, an ax in one hand, some gloves in the other, her red bandanna tied pirate style around her head. "Daylight's a-burning!"

I tumble out of the hammock and follow Ava to a mountain of wood behind the shed.

"Having dry cut wood is a matter of survival," starts Ava. "It's going to get real cold real fast."

Ava holds up the ax.

"Meet Beverly," she says.

"Beverly? You named your ax?"

"Shhhh," whispers Ava. "She's sensitive."

Oh. MyGod.

"Wait, you like, named your ax?" I repeat, amused.

"Hey." Ava shrugs. "Some people name their guinea pigs, I name my ax—big whoop. Now, let's get this party started. Ready?"

"Sure." I shrug.

"Splitting the wood and making sure we have dry wood in the cabin is going to be your responsibility."

Ava hands me the ax. It's heavier than I thought it

would be, and even though I'm strong, I struggle with it until Ava rearranges my grip.

"Like this," she says, wrapping my fingers properly around the worn wooden handle.

"Okay, so we're cool on your grip," says Ava. "Every season, my friend Tim comes by and dumps a cord of wood. It's basically wood that's cut to length but it still needs to be split so we can fit it in the woodstove. So what we . . ."

Ava continues to talk, but I kind of space out. I'm still back at Tim, wondering if he is the guy she was talking about. You know, the eco guy, the bush pilot, her *boyfriend*—

"Grace?" Ava looks pissed. "Are you listening?"

"Oh, sorry." I apologize and snap back to attention.

"All right," she continues. "So, this is nice hard wood. It's birch, and it burns really well because it's so dense." Ava knocks her hand against the wood and tosses it back in the pile. "Your job will be splitting the wood, stacking it, and making sure there's always a good supply in the cabin. Think you can handle that?"

I nod. *Sounds simple enough to me.*

"And just a heads-up here, splitting wood in a blizzard, with blustering snow and thirty mile per hour winds can be—" Ava looks at me like I'm in for a treat. "Let's just say it's not fun, so really, try and split the wood whenever there's a break in the weather, especially these next few weeks—trust me."

"Got it," I answer obediently. "No problem."

"Good," says Ava.

"Okay, so now I'm going to show you the proper way to split wood." She reaches for the ax and I hand it over.

"First, you need to always watch your toes and fingers, for obvious reasons." Ava props a log straight up on an old tree stump. "Step back," she warns.

I jump back a few feet and watch as Ava lifts the ax over her head, pausing for a second, the ax suspended high in the air. Then she does this primal scream–type war cry, which scares the crap out of me, and *Boom!* with one swing, she rips the log in two.

Whoa.

I don't know whether to laugh or run.

The whole primitive yelling thing was kind of—

Ava hands me back the ax. "Your turn," she says. "Oh, and the yell—just something someone passed on to me." She smiles and raises her eyebrows. "Supposed to help your Chi."

"Your Chi?"

"Your energy."

"Ooooh-kay," I say, laughing.

"Hey, don't knock it till you've tried it!" Ava bends down and takes hold of my right ankle, instructing me to move it until my legs are shoulder-width apart. "That's it. Perfect. Now, make sure to keep your feet planted firmly, and keep your eye on the log. It can be shifty."

I take a big breath, grip the ax with both hands, and hoist it above my head

"Let it out!" says Ava.

"I can't," I say, trying not to burst out laughing.

"Go on, Grace," cheers Ava.

And right at that moment, I almost just do it, but I start giggling, like, pee-in-my-pants kind of giggling, and I drop the ax onto the ground and fall down laughing.

Ava does not look quite so entertained by my exploits. She extends her hand and pulls me to my feet. "Easy does it," she says. "Come on, Grace this ax is sharp, okay? You can lose some fingers here—"

"Ah, yeah, that wouldn't be good," I say, trying not to laugh.

Finally, I compose myself, broaden my stance, and with both my hands gripped around the handle, raise the ax high above my head.

And what the heck—

I let out a long, high-pitched ear-piercing scream. It's a little more screechy than primal, but I do it, and then in one fluid motion, I bring the ax down and tear through the log.

Wow—

That felt kind of good.

"Nice!" says Ava, sounding impressed.

I shrug like it's no big deal.

"Okay, hotshot." Ava nods toward the mountain of logs. "Get at it," she says, walking away. "Oh, and Grace?"

"Yeah?" I look up.

"When you're done splitting the wood, bring some in. We're low in the cabin."

"No problem," I say with a swagger.

I mean, really, how hard can it be?

five hours later.

It can be hard.

Very hard.

Sweating, back-breaking, I've-never-been-this-physically-worn-out-in-my-entire-life kind of hard. This backwoods life is killing me. I lock myself in the bathroom, strip off my sweaty, sticky, smelly clothes, and step into the icy shower, where I stand directly under the spray and don't even flinch.

And don't you know it, Ava was right—

It feels good.

wardrobe.

I've been on *The Tonight Show* (three times), *David Letterman* (twice), and a guest of Katie Couric's (big tennis fan) at the Academy Awards, but tonight—

Tonight I'm going *bowling* and I can't figure out what to wear! I am in my bra and underwear, standing in my loft, careful not to hit my head on the ceiling, trying and retrying everything on, like I'm doing some strange tribal dance.

I put something on, take one look in the mirror and peel it off, and repeat this crazy striptease about a billion times, until I decide I'm hopeless and settle on jeans (comfortable), a T-shirt (casual), and one of Ava's handmade sweaters (hoping her splendor will rub off on me).

I fall back on my mattress and breathe deeply. I don't think I can ever remember being so excited and so nervous and so—

So completely awkward.

And I wish very hard that while I'm in Medicine Hat I can learn to somehow feel normal.

I am in the middle of reminding myself to smile and to not be a total dork, when I hear her.

Fisher.

"Hello?" she calls. "Ava? Emily? Anyone?"

I don't have to look.

I know it's her. Her voice is scratchy and friendly, and I don't know what comes over me, but I—

I just freeze.

Completely.

I crouch down behind the wooden dresser like a little girl, and I sit there—my heart beating fast—and listen to Fisher's footsteps as she walks around the cabin.

I don't know what my problem is.

Get a grip, Grace! I think, and will myself to stop being so afraid of everyone and everything.

"Hellooo?" she calls. "Anyone home?"

Bear comes bounding in the cabin and jumps up onto Fisher.

I can do it. I think. *Just be yourself.* A little voice in my head nudges me to my feet.

"Hey!" I say, looking down from the loft.

"Hey!" she says, beaming me this super-friendly smile that makes me feel like a complete idiot for hiding. Fisher's shiny black hair is pulled back into these crazy pigtails. Her light is abundant and enchanting, and as I watch her playfully tussle with Bear, I suddenly want nothing more than to be exactly like her.

I slide down the ladder, fireman style.

"Ready?" she asks, letting go of Bear.

"Yeah," I answer, a little too perky, a little too excited.

Calm down, Grace. "Um, I just better—" I pause for a second and try and think what the protocol is here. Do I check with Ava before I leave? She's not my mom, but she's still, as they say, the boss of me.

"Ava?" I call out, and at the very same moment, she strides in from the backyard.

"Hey, Fisher," says Ava.

"Hi," Fisher answers in a voice that is softer and more self-conscious than I have heard her use before.

We all kind of stand there.

It's a weird little moment—

"So—" I say, breaking the silence. "I guess we'll like, go?"

Ava leans in to hug me. It's a simple hug, a light kind of natural squeeze. And even though it catches me by surprise, it doesn't feel weird—

It feels perfectly normal.

"Be careful," she whispers before letting go.

"I will," I promise.

Ava and Bear stand guard at the front of the cabin and watch as Fisher and I bound down the hill.

"Midnight," Ava hollers. "Not a minute later."

the overlook.

Fisher's car is old. Ancient. And when I slide into the crusty vinyl passenger's seat, it occurs to me that, besides

Ava's truck, my pampered little butt has never ridden in anything like this.

"Sorry," says Fisher.

"About what?" I say, trying to be polite.

"My car." She glances at me as she drives. "I'm like, totally embarrassed that I have to pick you up in this, but it's all I can afford right now. I'm saving, though."

"It's fine," I say. "Really." I feel guilty for even noticing it was such a clunker. *Who really cares, right?*

"Well, whatever." She laughs. "It's my A.B. vehicle."

"A.B.?" I repeat.

Fisher pulls onto the main road. "It gets me from Point A to Point B, and really that's all you need, you know, to get where you're going." Fisher takes her eyes off the road and grins at me.

"Someday my ship will come in and I'll upgrade to one of those big black SUVs. You know, the kind you see all those celebrities driving on MTV. I know they're bad for the environment and everything, but whatever, right? I wouldn't mind having seat heat and those huge speakers in the back that make the whole car shake."

"No doubt," I agree. I agree like a big fat *faker*, like I wasn't just in a big black chauffeured SUV three days ago. The word *fraud* comes to mind. I swallow and try not to sweat.

"Um—" I search for something meaningful to say,

something that will peel the guilt away. "My dad used to say that people get too tied up in what kind of car they're driving, you know? That like, your identity shouldn't be tied up in what kind of car you drive."

"Well, your dad was smart." Fisher laughs. "Who wants to drive around in some fancy SUV," she jokes. "They probably suck."

"Yeah," I agree, laughing.

The weirdest thing is, I have never talked to anyone about my dad, and with Fisher—with Fisher, I've already brought him up twice.

"So," Fisher asks. "Where are you from, anyway?"

"California," I say. I say it and hope she doesn't ask too many questions.

"Wait." Fisher looks at me. "You left California for Medicine Hat?"

"Yeah, well, I don't know." I shrug. "It's kind of pretty here."

"Yeah, kind of," Fisher agrees. "In a dead-end-nice-if-you're-just-visiting kind of way," she says, bursting into a fit of laughter. "Just kidding!" Fisher turns the car off the road into what I think is a park. "I mean," she continues talking as she gets out of the car. "I teeter between wanting to go very far, far, faaaaar away from here, and not being able to imagine living anyplace else, but—"

As Fisher's talking I look around. We're the only car here.

"But what?" I ask, following her across the parking lot, through knee-high grass, to an old stone wall on the edge of a cliff. But Fisher doesn't finish. Instead, she hoists herself up onto the top of the wall.

I climb up too. We stand side by side.

The view is incredible.

With the light of the moon, you can see forever.

You can even see tiny little cars driving down Main Street.

And the ocean—

And the port, still busy, even at night.

"Wow," I say. "It's beautiful up here."

"I know." Fisher speaks softly. "This is where I come when I have some serious thinking to do."

For a few serene moments, the two of us just stand there. The only sound is the waves crashing into the seawall at the bottom of the cliff.

"Hey." Fisher points down below to the port. "See that boat?"

There are about a hundred boats, so I'm not sure which one she means.

"The one right there, see it? The one with the big boxy top. It's red. See the one I mean?"

"Oh, yeah," I say. I can't really, but I want to so

badly, I say I can. Then, thankfully, I do. I see it. It's an old wooden boat with a tattered flag blustering in the wind.

"That's my dad's."

"Your dad's a fisherman? That's so cool."

"Not really." Fisher tosses a small stone off the cliff. "It's a death wish is what it is."

"Um," I say, copying her and hurling a little rock down toward the ocean. "Why?"

"He's a tanner, which means he goes out in the worst weather for snow crab. It's just about the most dangerous job there is. People die like, all the time."

"Oh, man," I say. "What about your mom?"

Nice change of subject, right? Wrong.

"She split," says Fisher. She plunks down on her butt and dangles her legs off the side of the stone wall. I sit down too.

"Whatever, though." Fisher looks straight out at the ocean as she speaks. "I don't even remember her. She left when I was like, one."

I don't know what to say, so I don't say anything.

Fisher jumps to her feet. "Enough of my little sob story!" Her voice bright and bouncy again. "Hey, did you notice the range?"

"What range?" I jump back too.

Fisher takes my face in her hand and moves my

chin in the direction I'm supposed to be looking.

"See," she says, leaning her head in close to mine so we share the same view.

"Do you see them?"

"See what?"

"Right over there, see?" She points across the valley. That's right when I see them.

Two snowcapped peaks, so spectacular, so massive, that I'm embarrassed I've been here for three entire days and I haven't even noticed.

"It's like—" I search for the right description. "It's like a painting." I say. "Except we're—"

"In it!" finishes Fisher as she jumps down off the stone wall.

"So," she says.

"So, what?" I ask, leaping to the hard ground.

"So, now you know the official Medicine Hat make-out spot." She giggles and begins walking back. "Maybe you and your lover boy will come up here one night!"

My lover boy!

"Um, I don't know what you're—" I start, but it's useless, Fisher takes off running, and we race through the high grass to the car—

Giggling all the way.

two minutes later.

"Damn!" says Fisher, collapsing into the driver's seat, winded from our race. "You're pretty fast!"

"I guess," I say, and shrug as I slide back into the front seat.

"You're not even breathing heavy!" she jokes, still catching her breath.

"I'm not that fast." I lie. *I am that fast. Faster, even.*

"Well whatever, superstar," Fisher teases me and starts the car. "Back to my earlier point. It's natural, you know." She turns out of the parking lot. "Boy meets girl. Boy thinks girl is cute. Girl thinks Boy is cute. Hormones fly. It's Mother Nature!"

Gulp.

"I guess so," I say, blushing.

"So you like him, right?"

"Um," I start, but like—

I honestly think I'm like, socially retarded. My cheeks are flushed and my heart is beating fast and—

Fisher turns down Main Street. "I'll take the silly look on your face as a big fat YES." She smiles broadly. "And remember, that boy is my cousin, so let's make it a rule that from here on out we will not discuss his body or anything that would seriously gross me out."

"Okay," I crack up.

"Oh, and he's going to meet us, by the way."

"Who?" I say, kind of joking and kind of pretending that this isn't really all happening.

Fisher throws me a big you-know-who kind of grin.

I do know who.

I most certainly—

Do.

emmy lou.

The bowling alley is dark and smoky and it sort of smells like ashtray soup with a little stale beer stirred in. It's jam-packed and loud, and the bright neon lights make me feel like I'm in some old disco movie.

The first thing I notice is that every single person we pass says hi to Fisher.

Every single one.

The young guy behind the counter who gives us our shoes.

The lady at the bar, who waves and winks.

The three wrinkled elders in the lane beside us.

Everyone lights up when they see her. Like she's the mayor.

"Wow, you know everyone," I say, sticking my

enormous size-ten feet into the old leather bowling shoes.

"Yeah, well." Fisher grins like she's embarrassed. "It's a small town," she says.

"Still, you know everyone!"

"What*ever*." Fisher shrugs modestly. "Hey, come sit down." She slides into a chair at the scorer's table and pats the seat beside her. "I have something for you."

"For me?" I look surprised, as Fisher reaches into a brown paper bag, which I didn't even notice before. For a second I have this awful, sinking, disappointing flutter in my stomach. A this-must-be-the-part-where-I-find-out-my-new-best-friend-is-really-an-aloholic-and-she's-about-to-pull-out-a-flask-of-whisky kind of feeling.

Don't worry.

I'm completely wrong.

Not to mention completely guilt ridden for thinking such a thing.

Fisher does not pull a pint of whisky out of the brown paper bag.

No.

She pulls out a light pink bowling shirt with *Emmy Lou* stitched over the front pocket in dark blue thread.

It's adorable.

Totally adorable.

"Oh my God," I say, holding it up first, then slipping it on. "This is like—"

I'm speechless.

"Do you like it?" Fisher smiles proudly.

"Like it?" I twirl around. "I love it!"

Fisher reaches into the bag and pulls out another shirt, identical to mine, and slips it on. Her shirt has *Fisher Rae* stitched over the chest pocket.

"Where'd you get these?" I say, admiring the embroidery.

Fisher shrugs. "I made them."

"You made them!" I can't believe it.

Nobody has ever made me anything before.

"It's no big deal." She grins. "It took me like, two seconds."

"Emmy Lou," I read my name out loud. "I love it!"

Fisher giggles. "Yeah, well, I officially ordain you Emmy Lou. It's so you!"

"Thanks," I say.

Fisher jumps to her feet. "Enough of all this touchy-feely stuff! Let's bowl!"

"You go first!" she demands.

"Well, okay!" I squeal, spring to my feet, and hold my hand over the vent thingie like I've seen the bowlers do on TV. I pick up a ball from the rack and walk out onto the shiny lane and wiggle my butt before I go, making Fisher erupt in a hoot of laughter behind me.

The shoes are slick, and slide easily on the wooden floor. I take a few steps and glide as I extend my arm back. And even though I haven't bowled since Claire McLaughlin's fifth-grade birthday party, I hurl the ball so powerfully, so strong, that everyone in the place seems to stop what they are doing and look at our lane.

"Strike!" shrieks Fisher, leaping from her seat and hugging me like I just hit the jackpot.

Then those blinking flashing disco lights go crazy, and a siren roars, and the whole place breaks into applause!

It's like I've won the lottery or something.

In a way—

I think I have.

afterward.

We burst through the metal doors of the bowling alley, sweaty and giggling, but Teague-less. As in, he never showed. As in, I probably imagined that he even liked me in the first place. As in, I feel like a total loser for entertaining the possibility that Teague Denali, super hunk, was interested.

The ride back to Ava's is quiet. Not weird-quiet, just calm-quiet. Like you get when you've had way too much sugar and your body runs out of steam. Neither of us says much until Fisher drives up to the cabin and turns the engine off.

"Um, listen," she starts, sounding very serious. "I don't know where Teague was but, he's not usually like that. I mean, I'm sure something was going on or he would have—"

"Hey," I interrupt, embarrassed. "It's not like we're married!" I laugh, trying very hard to act like I don't really care, even though I totally do.

I pause for a second as I reach to open the car door.

"Thanks, Fisher." I smile. "I had so much fun."

"Yeah, probably 'cause you kicked my ass." She laughs. "Are you sure you aren't on the Pro Bowlers Tour?"

"Not even," I say, and try to change the subject. "I think it was my lucky shirt."

"Oh, Emmy Lou!" Fisher leans over and gives me a big hug before I swing the door open and step out into the night.

"Thanks." I wave and stand right there and watch until her car is out of sight.

Bear greets me in the darkness, and he doesn't even bark. He wags his tail and escorts me into the pitch-black cabin. Without thinking, I kneel down and scratch him behind his ears, the same way I have watched everyone else do it.

"Yeah," I whisper, and smile. Maybe I am a dog person after all. I pat his silky coat. "Yeah," I repeat softly. "You like that, don't you? Don't you, Bear?"

I throw an extra log on the fire and tiptoe past a sleeping Ava.

"Grace?" she mumbles. "Is that you?"

"Yeah," I say softly, freezing in my tracks. "It's me. I'm home, safe and sound."

"Good," Ava sighs. "Did you fill the locker?"

"Huh?" I whisper back, and try not to laugh.

"The milk—" she mumbles.

"The milk?" I repeat, my lips press together so my amusement doesn't escape.

"The milk, it's—" she mutters.

She's talking in her sleep!

"What milk?" I say, egging her on.

"It's in the art folder at the university."

"The art folder?" I'm laughing now.

Crying, even.

Ava sighs and rolls over, and I run for the back door.

Before I wake her with my laughing.

Deep, belly laughing.

Something I've noticed I've been doing a lot of these days.

adventure girl.

Outside, the sky looks fake.

Like I've walked onto a movie set and someone turned off all the lights except for the ten trillion white stars beaming through the ceiling.

That's when it hits me—

I will sleep outside!

Under the stars!

I do not stop to consider grizzly bears or caribou gobbling me up for their midnight snack. I don't think about the black flies or the rabid racoons or the bogeyman. No. One day of chopping wood and I've apparently transformed into Adventure Girl.

I don't even bother to change out of my clothes. I just slip back inside, grab the extra down sleeping bag out of the closet, and head for the hammock.

It takes a few minutes before I find the position that suits me, but when I do, I rock happily, nestled in my cocoon, and stare up into the night.

The stars are absurd.

Full of hope.

Of promise.

I've never felt closer to who I might be.

My wishes are numerous and easy.

The last one, I'll admit.

Begins with a—

T.

sunday.

In the morning I wake up to Bear licking my face.

As it turns out I am still not a dog person.

It's disgusting!

"Bear!" I push his wet, smelly nose out of my face and pull the sleeping bag up over my head.

But he won't quit.

"Bear, stop," I whine, my eyes still closed.

But he keeps nudging me.

"God, Bear, just leave me alone!" I say, this time opening my eyes.

Oh. My. God.

The universe does not mess around.

Teague.

He's standing, smiling—

Right there.

In front of me.

two minutes later.

Teague waits outside with Bear while I run like a girl who has never done this before (true, by the way), up to the loft, and peel off my sticky smoke-infested jeans, my adorable handmade *Emmy Lou* pink bowling shirt, and change into fresh clothes. I sprinkle a dab of Ava's home-made lavender oil behind my ears to dampen the fact that I smell like bowling alley. All and all, it takes me one minute to change. I think how great it feels to not worry about what I'm wearing, and run my fingers through my long blond hair before I remember, for like the billionth time, that I'm a redheaded punk girl, and catch a glimpse of my face in the tiny mirror above my dresser.

My eyes look different.

They're clearer and brighter, and the ruby in my nose makes me smile.

I hurry back downstairs, but put the brakes on when I fly by Ava in the kitchen.

"Well, good morning!" she says, handing me a cup of tea like she's the crew chief and I just drove in for my pit stop.

"Thanks," I take a sip.

Ava smiles and nods out the window. "I see you have some company."

"Yes, I do," I answer, and feel my cheeks blush. "Um, is it like, okay if we go for a walk?"

"A walk, huh?" Ava leans back against the counter and folds her arms over her chest, and for a second I have this sinking feeling that she's not going to let me go. Then she breaks into a smile. "Be back before dark—"

"It's like, morning," I say. "I mean, I don't think I'll be gone all day."

"Ummm, no—" Ava mimics me in this Valley Girl voice. "It's like, noon!" She laughs.

"Noon!" My jaw drops.

I've never slept this late in my life.

"I guess all this fresh air is wearin' you out!" She winks. "Or maybe it was your time with Beverly."

"Maybe," I say, remembering all the wood I chopped.

Just at this moment I catch a glimpse of Teague playing with Bear by the hammock, and in an impulsive burst of appreciation for my recent good luck, I throw my arms around Ava. "Thanks!" I tell her before I let go and head out the door.

"Grace." Ava calls out my name, *my real name,* loudly, and when I turn back to look, both of us realize the error.

"Emily," she says, like nothing happened.

They must have taught her this, nerves-of-steel stuff in the

FBI. "There's a cold front headed this way. Are you sure you don't want to take a sweater or something?"

"No thanks, I'm good." I wave and turn toward Teague, but before I reach him, I glance back at Ava leaning in the doorway, holding her tea.

Her face—

She looks happy.

I'm beginning to get the feeling that she likes having me around.

in the woods.

Teague blazes the trail, and I follow close behind at a pretty fast clip.

"Hey," I call ahead. "Um, is there a particular reason we are going so fast?"

Teague keeps going. I don't know if he doesn't hear me or what, but he just glides ahead, ducking under errant branches, hurdling over fallen tree trunks. He is nimble and quick, and in these woods he seems very much at home.

After forty-five minutes of our little game of cat and mouse, I finally catch up to him, already sitting down on a flat rock on the edge of the river, drinking from a canteen.

"It's about time," he says, grinning. "I was almost going to give up on you." He winks.

I crumple onto the rock, right beside him. For the first time, since the other day, we are touching. My shoulder is brushing up against his and there is an electric current running through the air that seems to be hogging all the attention.

Thankfully, Teague speaks before I faint. "Water?" he asks, offering up his canteen.

"Sure, thanks," I say, taking a swig and catching my breath.

"So." His eyes widen. "You're in pretty good shape."

"Apparently not," I say sarcastically. "Not good enough."

"No, you are." He smiles.

Dimples. Major dimples.

"It's true. Really." He nods as he speaks. "I don't think I've ever met anyone who can keep up with me like that."

"Yeah, well." I smile back, but instead of taking the compliment like my mom always says I really need to learn to do, I brush it off with a lame attempt at humor.

"It was a matter of survival," I say. "I just didn't want to get abandoned in the woods."

Teague stands and thoughtfully extends his hand to pull me up. His hand is warm and muscular, and we both hold on a second longer than we have to.

"Thanks," I say, letting go first.

"Hey, you know I would never leave you out here by yourself," he says. "I mean, just know that, okay?"

"Oh, I was just joking," I tell him.

"Yeah, I know, but still—" He gets kind of serious. "These woods, they're fun but they can be dangerous. It's kind of an unwritten rule to either tell someone where you're going, or make sure when you do go out, you go with someone else."

"Okay." I shrug, touched by his concern for my personal welfare.

"Emily," he says. "Be careful, okay? This isn't California."

"O-kaaaay," I say, smiling. "I promise."

"Good," says Teague. Then he takes off, springing like a leapfrog from rock to rock until he's standing in the middle of the river, where he pauses momentarily on top of a large boulder and cups his hands over his mouth. "Come on!" he shouts back.

Now, normally—

Normally I would think twice about this bold little acrobatic adventure. Normally a thousand reasons why I should err on the side of caution would flood my mind—

Do not break your wrist.

Do not get your clothes wet.

Do not fall desperately in love when you know you'll be leaving!

But ever since I've been in Alaska, I'm surprising myself. And this time—

This time is no exception.

three minutes later.

"That's it!" yells Teague. "You're almost there. Nice!"

I straddle my feet from rock to rock until, by some major miracle, I reach the other side (wrist unbroken, clothes dry, major feelings of affection).

"Wow!" I say, looking back at the current. "I can't believe I just crossed that."

"Well, you did," says Teague. "It's not something you'd want to do if the current were much stronger—that would be dangerous—but this—" He smiles and shrugs. "This is just fun."

"Yeah it is," I agree. "So what's next?" I say, wanting more.

Teague looks up the river, and then back at me.

"I want to show you something," he tells me.

"What do you want to show me?" I say, surprising even myself at how hopelessly flirty I sound.

"You'll see," he says. "But you have to promise me something."

I tilt my head and twinkle my eyes. "You sure are making me promise a lot!" I say.

Teague grins. "No, honestly, promise you won't show anyone. It's like—"

He pauses.

"Top secret?"

"Right." He smiles. "Top secret."

"Do you want to seal this little agreement with a kiss?" I ask.

No-o-o-o-o-o. I think it, though. I think it, and nod. Yes. And I follow him. I follow him along the rocks beside the river, until he stops in his tracks and turns to me with his finger over his lips.

"Shhh." He motions and nods up into the canopy of trees we are standing under.

I look up.

"What?" I whisper.

Teague ducks behind me, right behind me—so close I can feel his breath on my neck.

I am shivering, and it's not because I'm cold.

"See it?" he whispers.

I squint up into the tree and try to concentrate on whatever it is I am supposed to see and not on Teague's soothing voice and that fact that I'm melting.

"Um," I say softly, "what am I loo—"

But before I get the words out, I see it.

An eagle.

It's massive, with a white head and white tail

feathers and bright yellow feet, like you see in pictures.

"It's a bald eagle," he whispers. "They like to wait here by the river and feast on salmon carcasses."

"Salmon carcasses?" I whisper.

"Yeah," he says. "After the salmon spawn, they die."

"They just die?" I sigh.

"Yeah," breathes Teague.

Goose bumps.

"There will be a lot more up here soon," he says softly. "They come in droves, hundreds of them in November, when food is scarce."

"Oh," I say, and stand openmouthed as the bird launches off its perch and soars. Its wingspan must be at least three feet on either side. I feel like I'm in a *National Geographic* special.

"Did you know they mate for life?" says Teague, still whispering.

"No, I didn't," I say, half listening and half noting that Teague seems to be a genius.

"Yeah." He nods. "And when they dive for prey they can get up to a hundred miles per hour."

"Wow," I say softly. "Why are we still whispering?" I laugh. "And was that it, the eagle? Was that the secret?"

Teague doesn't say anything. He just ducks under a

branch, up a well-worn path, away from the river and into the woods, and motions for me to follow.

the secret.

It's a cabin. The cutest cabin you've ever seen. On a little, meadowy knoll overlooking the river.

It's so sweet! Like a real-life dollhouse.

"This is it," says Teague, jumping up onto the miniature front porch.

"I love it," I say, leaping up to join him. "It's adorable! How did you find it?"

"Find it?" He laughs. "I built it."

My jaw drops.

Teague nods and smiles modestly.

"Like, by yourself?"

I can't believe it.

"With my own two hands," he says, grinning in such a way that I can tell he is pleased that I'm impressed.

"But, like—" I look off the porch to the river, the meadow, and the lush forest surrounding us. "Whose land is this?"

"Mine," says Teague.

"You *own* your own land?" I say, surprised. I mean, he's only sixteen.

"My dad gave it to me."

"Your dad just like, gave you your own land?"

"Well." Teague smiles. "He left it to me."

"Left it to you?"

I don't get it.

"When he passed," says Teague.

"Ohhhh," I say, and feel like an idiot.

"It's okay," Teague opens the door and motions for me to follow. "He died a long time ago."

"Teague—" I say. "This is beautiful." I step inside and look around at the golden maple floors and the wall of windows with daylight spilling in. It's simple. And sweet. Just a small woodstove, some firewood stacked against the wall, a few jugs of water, and a rolled-up blanket. It smells like wood smoke.

I walk back out and sit down on the front steps, worn and smooth.

"So," I say, squinting into the sun. "Do you come here a lot?"

"Not as much as I'd like to." Teague plops down next to me. "You know, school, chores, taking care of my brother."

"You have a little brother?"

"Older," Teague sighs. "Major screwup."

"Sorry," I say.

"Don't be, but—" Teague pauses.

"But what?"

"Well, that's kind of why I brought you out here. I want to apologize."

"Apologize?"

"Yeah, um, I felt so bad about standing you and Fisher up last night, but my brother sort of—" he starts, like he's about to explain, but then changes his mind. "Let's just say he's a major screwup and leave it at that."

I nod.

He nods.

He smiles at me.

There's something about this land that releases me from the obligation of words. Maybe it's the birds rustling in the woods, or the river down below. But it's peaceful. Tranquil, even.

"Also, I wanted to apologize for not dropping your bike off the other day. My brother, he—" Teague looks off into the woods and then back at me. "I don't want you to get the wrong impression about me."

"Well, I don't," I say, and smile softly.

Teague just kind of looks into my eyes and smiles the gentlest smile, and I think, this is it, you know?

This is what all the fuss is about.

timing.

We are sitting on the porch. Still. The sun is setting, the sky is this lush deep pink hue, my heart is beating out of my chest, and I am actually thinking—

Could my first kiss be any more perfect?

I'm actually thinking—

Do I like, lean in? Do I close my eyes?

Do I open my mouth?

But no—

No.

Teague jumps to his feet.

"Oh man," he says, looking somewhat alarmed. "It's going to get dark soon."

He reaches out and pulls me to my feet.

This time I go first.

My legs fall easily, swiftly, elegantly into a gentle steady pace.

It's instinctive and joyful.

And it feels as if my feet

hardly

touch

the ground.

part three

"Hello, sun in my face
Hello, you who made the morning
and spread it over the fields. . . .
Watch, now, how I start the day
in happiness, in kindness."
—Mary Oliver

three weeks later.

I learn quickly that there is no place on this island for fashion statements. It's cold. The kind of cold that seeps underneath your skin and leaves marks on your face and makes you obsessively vigilant about wearing a hat. Not just for decoration either, a warm hat with fur inside and aviator-style flaps that I tug down over my ears. I have gone from Prada to Patagonia, from cute spaghetti-strapped tops and cropped baby tees to long underwear and thick wool sweaters. The best thing of all is nobody cares what I'm wearing. Nobody. In Medicine Hat it is cool to bundle up, to be warm, to, as Ava likes to say, "Take responsibility for your comfort."

So I choose function over fashion.

And it suits me just fine.

I whittle my mornings to a science. I chop and stack the wood (with Beverly), I make myself breakfast (pancakes with real maple syrup), and skip a shower in favor of a washcloth, which I hang over the woodstove and roast like a piece of meat, carrying it piping hot, tossing it between my hands like a hot potato, sprinting all the way into the bathroom, where I run it over my skin. Maybe you don't want to picture me naked, washing. Maybe it's, as they say, too much information, but I share this to say that—I, girl of five-star hotels, queen of fluffy white towels, she who (don't laugh) has her own line of cosmetics—takes such joy in simple pleasures.

Sometimes I even do it twice.

Remarkably, I have grown to appreciate wearing the same thing every day. It's easy. It's simple. There are no agonizing choices to be made. I slip into my long underwear, jeans, T-shirt, wool sweater, and Ava's hand-stitched sealskin boots. I do not toy with the weather gods. In Medicine Hat, those pink furry UGG boots that models wear in L.A. would not last one single day.

It's still dark out when I run down the quarter mile stretch of driveway to catch the bus. I do not leave my parka unzipped, or my hood down, or the tiniest piece of skin exposed. I am surprised that somehow I am no longer scared of the dark. It's eerily peaceful at seven in the morning, so I saunter. I stroll. I listen to trees bend and lean and sing their songs.

Wrapped up like a polar explorer, I delight in my self-reliance. My unaided mission.

I feel native, indigenous, clever.

Born to be this girl.

Born to be.

school.

On the bus, I knit.

Ava taught me.

I knit all the way up the gravel road to Egegik Senior High School. Then I pile off the bus with all the other kids, and inhale the mountains, the pine trees, the thundering waterfalls.

Egegik is an Aluttiq word that means "between the rivers," which is where the weathered wooden school sits, tucked at the base of the mountains, nestled on a quiet stretch of green. The building looks more like a barn than a school. But inside it's light and airy, with tall generous windows, and walls painted warm, carroty hues that kind of make you feel like you walked into an episode of *Trading Spaces* and you got the plucky young designer with the Southern accent and the big smile. It's cheerful. It's clean. There's a gym, the only hot showers on-island, three small classrooms, and a kitchen, where we take turns cooking lunch for the entire school, serving the food and washing the dishes.

All six teachers line up at the door and greet us each morning. Like the receiving line at a wedding.

Aleut, Yupiks, and a handful of white kids file in.

There is no distinction, no partiality.

We are all greeted, welcomed, embraced.

It took me a few days to get used to.

"Hi, Emily," they say. "Greetings!" (Hug, hug, hug.)

My classmates are equally gracious.

And I can tell by their frayed clothes, by the look in their eyes—

They value this school.

This place.

Like a prize.

snow.

I am walking to Sadie's with Fisher when the first blizzard roars in. I feel like I'm inside one of those little globe thingies that people collect as souvenirs—my world has been shaken and stirred and all of a sudden snow pours down on us like confetti. Fisher is amused at my fascination with the fluffy white stuff. I chase it. I stick my tongue out and taste it. Fisher does too, mocking me at first, and then falling under the spell of the surreal wonder dust blanketing the earth, our faces, and the tips of our noses.

We fall down laughing.

The two of us.

Lapping up snow.

Succumbing to fits of absolute silliness.

At Sadie's, I sit across from Fisher at "the table." The same one in the corner where I sat that first day with Teague, who, thanks for asking, besides furtive hallway glances and idle chitchat (the weather, homework, diminishing sunlight), I have not hung out with since the day he showed me his cabin. He leaves school after lunch and heads straight to the docks, where he works for commercial fisheries that pay him cash (so says Fisher), to help haul in salmon, herring, halibut—whatever the season calls for. After that (I am told by his obliging cousin), my *lover boy* reports directly to his second job at the processing plant on the edge of town. The fact that I have enough money (more, really) to pull out my checkbook and BUY the processing plant is something that crosses my mind.

Something that leaves a knot in my stomach and makes me want to crawl into a hole.

I feel awful just thinking about it.

later.

When Teague steps into Sadie's and settles into the chair next to mine, it is virtually impossible for me to concentrate on anything besides the fact that his knee is scraping against mine—certainly not on my geometry homework.

"Hey, stranger," he says, politely removing his wool cap and setting it on the table.

He reeks of fish.

"Hey," I say.

"How are you?" he says.

More knee knocking.

"Good, good," I say, tilting my head and batting my eyes like a mutant-teenage Barbie and wondering if this ever gets easy.

"So—" He leans back in his chair.

"So." I smile.

"Um." He leans in.

I'm melting.

Melting.

"So, are you going to that party?" he asks.

"What party?" I lie. Fisher has told me all about *the party*. She's talked about it for three days. It's at Henry Eagle's cousin's boyfriend's sister's house.

"Henry's," he says. "You going?"

"Well, I think so." I shrug. "Are you?"

Teague shakes his head. "Not really my scene, but—"

"But?"

"Well, maybe I'll—" He stands up and puts his hand on my shoulder. "Maybe I'll see you," he says.

"Yeah, umm." I'm clumsy, distracted by the ten thousand mini-tremors shooting through my body. "Umm, I hope so."

"Bye, Em," he says, backpedaling as he leaves, muffin in hand.

Don't think I'm not watching.

After the door to Sadie's clangs shut, he looks back over his shoulder, a full shine in his eyes, and beams me the most beautiful smile.

I open my geometry textbook and stare blankly at the assignment. I am in a total daze.

A wraith of Teague's fish odor drifts by. Fish odor, in general, is not the nicest smell, not something I would normally find pleasant, sweet, perfume-like. But on this day I take a second sniff.

Essence of Teague.

I inhale.

two hours later.

It's dark. I have to catch the last bus home. I stuff my books in my backpack while Fisher reviews our evening agenda.

"I'm going to pick you up at eight."

"Eight." I nod. "Got it." I zip up my parka.

"And wear warm clothes because we're riding my dad's Honda."

"Honda?"

"You know," says Fisher. "Snowmobile."

"Cool!" I pull my hat down over my ears. "So wait, where exactly is this party, anyway?"

"Oh, it's on Main Street, by the Washeteria." Fisher's voice is suddenly low and whispery, and something about it gives me a nervous jolt.

Let's be honest here: my party experience is limited to the Wimbledon Ball, the *Vanity Fair* Oscar Gala, and ESPN's ESPY bash. I have never been to this kind of thing, and I can tell by the look in Fisher's eyes that this is not your typical spin-the-bottle-variety get-together.

But whatever, right?

I wanted the *teenage experience.*

To be regular.

To blend in.

I take a deep breath. "I'll be ready!" I say.

I fly out of Sadie's with a glint in my eyes.

I'm young! I think, dashing to the bus.

I'm free, I think, settling into my seat.

I'm in Medicine Hat, I think, running up the driveway to the cabin.

What could go wrong?

what could go wrong.

I have to lie to Ava.

She's on the couch reading when I tell her.

"Bowling?" she says, peering over her glasses. "Just be back by midnight. You know the drill."

when I leave.

The lump of guilt in my throat is large, but apparently not large enough to stop me from running down the hill and sliding onto the back of my waiting getaway vehicle.

Fisher hands me my helmet.

"Ready?" she yells, gunning the engine before I even answer.

I hold on for dear life as Fisher projects us down the bumpy winding driveway, onto the main road. She drives like a cowgirl, coaxing the five-hundred-pound beast up icy hills, hurtling us down the dark side of the mountain into town.

party.

The house is falling to pieces.

Think crime scene.

Think crack house.

Think bad idea.

But I'm needy and ripe, greedy for my youth, and I follow Fisher up the icy steps like a starved stray puppy.

Inside, I gag. It reeks. Like someone peed on the dark shaggy carpet and never cleaned it up. I duck my head back outside and take a big gulp of air and hold my breath like I'm diving for a coin at the bottom of a pool. I hold it like that till I can't hold it any longer, as I tag behind Fisher, through the packed hallway, past shadowed faces, past people I have never seen, people I do not recognize, people who look older, wilder—

High.

My eyes adjust to the hazy smoke-filled rooms as I duck under tufts of cigarettes, through faint trails of marijuana, past couples making out in the corner.

My Perfect Girl voice is freaking out.

Be safe Grace! Be responsible. Do the right thing. Blah, blah, blah.

I push the nagging worried warnings away, I push Little Ms. Perfect to the depth of my conscience. I stuff her and her panic, her unease, her predictability under the farthest corner of my brain.

Hidden.

Out of sight.

And just like that, I am suddenly, strangely, maniacally overcome with the overwhelming desire to do the wrong thing.

Absolutely, entirely,

wrong.

the wrong thing.

I follow Fisher through jammed hallways, past loud people, laughing people, past older guys who purposefully chafe against my body—

Older guys whose eyes chase me, whose looks linger. Nothing I am not used to, but for some reason, tonight I let their eyes slide off me. I'm Teflon Girl. I straighten my posture and stare them down. I keep my elbows cocked, ready to rumble. *I can do this*, I tell myself, and shake my head because, really, I'm pathetic, I'm crazy, and I'm giving myself a pep talk to make it through a party.

It's a party, Grace!

Loosen up, for goodness' sake.

We hide our parkas under a coffee table in a back room, then Fisher grabs my hand, smiling back at me as she leads, pulling me along as if I'm a blind girl and she's my guide. We slide through gaps of space, sandwiched between sweaty bodies, inching our way down a stairwell to a basement more packed, more crowded, more dark, with tall black speakers thundering so loud, the walls are shaking. I drop Fisher's hand and plug my ears. The ground is vibrating, rumbling, springing up and down like one of those bouncy gymnastic floors.

And, surprise-surprise—

Ms. Perfect.

She's back.

Uninvited.

Voicing her misgivings inside my head.

This place is way too crowded.

An accident waiting to happen—

What if there is a fire? What if the floor caves in?

You are going to get trampled to death—

TENNIS SENSATION FOUND DEAD IN RUBBLE!

"Fisher, wait—" I call ahead.

"Fisher!" I repeat, this time louder. It's no use.

If this were a movie, you would only hear the music and see a close-up of my wide-open mouth, my moving lips, my empty, pitiable, plea drowned out by deafening, pulsating, music.

Poof.

She's gone.

one minute later.

I stand against the wall, fold my arms over my chest, and close my eyes. I take deep breaths, the kind I imagine you should take when you are about to have your second nervous breakdown of your not yet–adult life. The new me, the one I like, the one I have most recently grown to be. I watch her. I watch her float, hover, drift above me— My voice of reason has abandoned ship.

Ms. Perfect has quit her post.

If you are going to be an idiot she tells me, *you're on your own.*

God.

I know!

I think I've gone nuts.

Maybe I'm hallucinating.

Maybe I'm crazy.

All I can say is, I'm having one of those moments where you know that what you are about to do is not you. Not wise. Where you know that what you are about to consume, touch, feel, will undoubtedly cause you harm.

You know this.

You totally know.

Then—

You do it anyway.

sex on the beach.

I stride to the makeshift bar with intention, with focus.

Before I change my mind.

"What is this?" I ask this girl with short knotty hair who is pouring a pitcher into blue plastic cups.

"Sex on the Beach," she shouts over the music, and flashes me a smile. She is friendly and perky and she wears glitter on her eyelids. Her smile disarms me. Like the fact that she's nice somehow makes what I'm about to do acceptable, normal, no big deal.

"Sex on the Beach?" I speak over the music.

"IT'S VODKA MOSTLY," she answers, bobbing her head to the beat while she pours. The liquid is fluorescent yellow, and she meticulously fills every cup until the table looks like a modern design of concentric circles, glowing like toxic waste.

"Is this, like, free?" I say.

She cups her hand up to her ear. "What?"

"IS THIS FREE?" I repeat.

"Yeah it is!" She hands me one.

"Knock yourself out!" she says.

This is not a proud moment.

It's impulsive and stupid and not who I want to be.

I don't even really think about Teague, or Ava, or anyone but me. I certainly don't do any of those things they tell you in D.A.R.E.

I do not walk away.

I do not change the subject.

I do not blame a non-present third party.

I do not say no.

Just this one time, right?

Live a little, right?

I'm young, right?

I take a swig.

Okay, not a swig—

I down the entire cup.

I down it like medicine.

My face contorts and shudders as I swallow.

It's disgusting.

It burns.

After that—

I have another.

three drinks later.

I'm drunk, smashed, three sheets to the wind.

It does not take long.

I dance like a wild child. Sweat pours off my head

like I'm the star of my own music video. I shake my butt, my head, I close my eyes. I am uninhibited, loose, easy, free, and as I whirl and twirl, I watch in horror as the contents of my cup spill all over the girl standing next to me.

"Imsosorry." I'm slurring.

The music stops.

Well, it doesn't really stop.

But I do.

She does.

The fluorescent yellow liquid—formally known as my fourth Sex on the Beach—is splattered all over the front of her blouse like a first-grade finger-painting masterpiece.

She's enraged.

Livid.

Hysterical.

Her mouth is moving and something is coming out, but I'm having trouble focusing, catching up with the words.

"What the hell is your problem?

"Can you not walk?

"Are you retarded?"

My throat tightens.

My heart trembles.

"I'msoooosorry," I say.

I'm talking too loud.

Too drunk. My voice is irritating and foreign, and I'm woozy times three. And the girl, yes, the one who is going to kill me. She strips. Stands there in front of me, in the middle of the basement dance floor, and peels her shirt over her black ponytail and strips down to a lacy purple bra. She holds up her soaked shirt and waves it in my face.

"How do you expect me to clean this?"

There is now an audience.

A circle of spectators, egging her on.

And as I stare at their eyes, their blank blurry faces, I have this drunken epiphany.

For the first time in my life.

Not one of them.

Not one single person,

Is cheering—

for me.

Ten seconds later.

A scary-looking dude with a shaved head, pockmarked skin, and an eagle tattooed on his neck steps into the circle like a gang leader from *West Side Story*.

"What's the problem?" he says, sliding his arm around the waist of the girl in the bra.

I really need to leave.

Fast.

I glance around the room.

I search for Fisher.

For Teague.

For my glass slipper—

For the first time since I left New York, I think of Big T, and wish he would magically materialize, whisk me away.

Save me.

"Um," I say, stumbling. "Look." I try again. "I really didn't mean to, like—"

"You look." Tattoo Guy thrusts his finger up to the tip of my nose. "You need to watch where the f— "

He pauses to hack up a phlegmy guttural cough, which he discharges into his blue plastic cup.

My lower lip begins to quiver.

Breathe, Grace.

Breathe.

No! Leave Grace.

Leave!

I turn, but he grabs my wrist.

Tattoo Guy.

His hand is sticky, sweaty, stronger than mine.

"Not so fast, Freak," he says.

Freak?

He leers at me. "Who do you think you are?"

Maybe it's the vodka, or that his grip is hurting me.

I snap.

Like the Incredible Hulk, minus the green paint and the green hair.

The veins in my neck even pop out.

"Let. Go." I say. I say it firmly, lucidly.

I over-annunciate.

"Let." (long pause) "Go."

But Tattoo Guy doesn't let go. He just stares and smiles and tightens his grip. And the next thing I know, I let loose this primal, screaming roar. Like I'm chopping with the ax—

With Beverly.

"LET. GO!" I stare back into his seedy dark eyes, and with all my might, wrench my hand free.

then.

I run.

I run like I'm being chased.

I push and shove and plow my way through the rooms.

I'm a madwoman—

A runaway train.

I hurl doors open, barging in on dim silhouettes of couples on beds, on floors, on kitchen counters, until I find her. Fisher. Sitting on a washing machine, making out with a skinny guy with a yellow mohawk. If I weren't bawling, it would actually be funny, but I am, crying I mean. My tears are messy. Falling fast.

"Em?" Fisher calls toward me. "Is that you?"

"I—" (Sob.) "I just—"

She doesn't wait for me to explain.

She doesn't stop for introductions.

She doesn't hesitate.

No panic.

No alarm.

Fisher jumps off the washer, wraps her hand around mine, leads me up a flight of stairs, through a crowded hallway, into the dark room where we stashed our coats, grabs mine first, then hers, all the while holding my hand with a tight-clutching-don't-worry-I-won't-let-go kind of grip, until, together, we burst out the front door, into the darkness.

The frigid air shocks my skin, my face, my wet cheeks. We descend the front steps in one icy leap and run straight down the center of the empty street.

getaway.

On the snowmobile, I am weeping, sobbing, blubbering under my helmet, pressed up against Fisher's back. I hug her like my life depends on it, over icy bumps, around the bends.

At the Lookout, we sit side by side on the stone wall, wrapped up like Russian soldiers, our furry hats flop over our ears. We sit there, the two of us, looking down at the harbor, at the boats, the sea. Snow gushing out of the sky so fast and steady it doesn't seem real.

Fisher's arm is weaved through mine, partly holding me up, partly comforting me.

"I should never have taken you to that party," she sighs. "It was sketchy—"

"Totallysketchy," I blurt out much too loudly, wiping my nose with the back of my mitten and snorting back snot in an incredibly unladylike manner.

"Waitasecond!" I say, trying to sound like I'm not pitifully drunk. "Whowasthedudewiththemohawk!"

Fisher shakes her head. "Now you know," she says.

"Knowwhat?"

I watch her breath shoot out into the darkness. "I occasionally exhibit a serious case of extremely bad judgment. Um, speaking of which—" Fisher turns to me, her eyes kind of wide. "I didn't know you were into drink-ing," she says with a shrug. "I just didn't like, have that feeling about you. I mean, not that it's a big deal—it's just, well, I don't drink and I mean it's not that I want to tell you what to do, it's just that—" She looks away, off the ledge, toward the sea. "It's just, it's kind of like, you know, been there, done that—"

I'm feeling dizzy. I lay back flat on the wall and shut my eyes.

"Idon'tdrink," I mumble into outer space.

My head is suddenly pounding.

"You sure about that?" Fisher looks down at me, passed out on the wall, amused by my incoherence.

I open my eyes.

I open my mouth.

I trap snow and taste it.

"Thatwaslike—" I pause. "Thatwasthefirsttimeinmy-entirelife."

Fisher lays back too, both of us lie there quietly, snow tumbling down on us.

"Em?"

"Em!" I turn my head sideways and look at Fisher like she's crazy.

"That's your name, isn't it?" Fisher laughs.

"OHRIGHT!" I shoot upright, sobered by my slipup.

"Whoa," says Fisher, grabbing my arm. "You okay?"

"Yeah." I lie.

Fisher sits up, too, wisely still holding my arm, not trusting my balance. "This whole night was all my fault. We should have left as soon as we walked in, it's just, well, I guess I wanted to impress you, you know?"

"Impress me?"

"Yeah, you know, you're from *California* and here we are in the middle of nowhere, and—" Fisher takes a big long breath. I watch the vapor, the warm air, leave her mouth like smoke. "I'm sorry," she says. "God, I'm just—"

"NOI'MSORRY," I jump in, too loud still, which makes us both crack up.

Fisher gets up and pulls me to my feet. The two of us stand on the wall overlooking everything.

"You know—" starts Fisher. "None of those people, I mean practically none of the people at the party were from here. They took the ferry in from Hawkshead."

"Yeah," I say, like I know what I am talking about even though I obviously don't.

I stumble, woozy, and Fisher catches me.

"Whoa!" I say, and giggle because I'm shouting at the stars and the moon, and my voice is echoing off the cliff. "And it's not your fault it's *my* fault!" I say.

"What?" This time, Fisher looks at me like I'm crazy.

"I lied."

"Lied?" Fisher scrunches up her eyebrows. "To who?"

"Ava." I burp.

"Oh boy," she says.

midnight.

Bless her heart, Fisher helps me all the way to the door.

"You got it from here?" she asks.

"I GOT IT," I whisper in her ear like a little kid telling a secret. "You'rethebest," I say.

I stumble alone into the cabin, and try to walk like I'm not drunk. Like I'm not terribly drunk.

Bear is barking.

Yipping and yapping.

He knows what I've done.

"Shhh," I beg.

"Bear!" I put my finger to my mouth like he can actually understand me. "Shhhhh."

"Grace?"

Shoot.

I crash into the table. "Whoops!"

"It's me." I soften my voice. "I'm hooome," I sing.

I make it up the ladder to my loft.

I make it into my bed.

Fully dressed.

I pull the covers up around my chin.

I think, Hey, whatever, maybe drinking wasn't such a bad idea, right?

It was kind of an experiment.

I lived and I learned.

Right?

Wrong.

Wrong.

Wrong.

I fall off my bed, trip going down the ladder of the loft, barf (three times), splattering the contents of my stomach all over the outhouse, where I sit, holding my head, crying like a baby, wishing the room would stop spinning.

Wishing I hadn't done what I did.

two hours later.

Waking up Ava is not one of my better ideas.

But I'm desperate.

I think I might be dying.

"Ava," I say, sniveling, snot hanging out of my nose.

Ava speaks into her pillow. "Grace?" she says.

"Ava." I flop down on the couch. "The room, it's spinning, and I'm, like—"

"Have you been drinking?" Her words are muffled, gargled, distorted in my mixed-up brain.

My head is pounding.

And okay, I'm a little dramatic.

"Yeah," I say softly under my breath. "But like, the room is spinning, and, like—" I snort back my runny nose. "I think I might be really sick."

Ava doesn't budge.

Doesn't even move to look at me.

I don't think I have ever felt worse.

I sit there trembling, whimpering, waiting for her to scold me, yell at me, save me from myself.

I watch her back rise and fall.

Minutes go by.

"Ava?" I whisper. "Ava?"

"Clean it up," she says.

She doesn't say another word.

four a.m.

In the outhouse, on my hands and knees, I attempt to scrape my frozen vomit off the floor. Chunks of dinner mixed with fluorescent lumps of Sex on the Beach. I plug my nose and hold my breath. I'm dizzy still, and the outhouse stinks.

I'm hopeless, desperate, full of anxiety.

I am disgusted with myself.

I can't believe I did this

I will never drink again.

You are such a friggin' idiot, Grace!!

Inside the cabin, I strip off my smelly clothes and step into the shower.

I pour on way too much soap.

I scrub with my washcloth.

Harder than normal.

I scour every inch of me and stand motionless under the icy cold spray.

Until I'm numb.

Naked and numb.

Wishing I could wash this night away.

in the morning.

I hear Ava.

Talking into her satellite phone.

I'm pretty sure it's my mom.

Great. Terrific, I think, and burrow my head under my pillow. My mother's displeasure is seriously more than I can stomach.

Ava speaks into the phone louder than normal.

I'm pretty sure she wants me to hear.

"Yes," she is saying. "Yes, I agree."

Agree what?

Ava laughs. "Exactly! That's right."

What's right?

"Okay, I'll call her as soon as I hang up. She's great. Fantastic. I've been seeing her for, well, since everything happened."

Who is her and what happened?

"Okay." Ava pauses to write something down.

"Got it," she says as she writes.

"Yes, still sleeping. I know!"

Long pause.

"Great, yes, uh-huh," says Ava.

"You too, Lily—"

My mom. I knew it.

"You too," Ava sighs. "I know, yes, I hope so too."

I can hear the keys on Ava's fancy phone beep.

She's dialing.

"Hi, this is Ava. I hope it's not too early to be calling?"

Long pause.

"That's right, yes, did she talk to you? How does after school sound?" Ava scribbles something down. I can hear the pencil strokes.

"Four then, and is it okay if she just comes in by herself? Good, good—" Another pause. "Thank you, Theona, thanks so much."

Theona?

I peer over the railing of my loft and my eyes meet Ava's. It's like she has a sixth sense or something.

"Yes, that's right, short red hair," she says, looking up at me. "Oh, yes," she says, her eyes beaming me a hint of a smile. "I think you will enjoy knowing her too."

snowshoe.

"Let's go. You need fresh air!" Ava tells me before she bounds straight out the back of the cabin, poles in hand, snowshoes strapped on, striding, gliding, dancing across the crusty top layer of ice.

"Come on, Grace!" she shouts back. "A little exercise will do you a world of good."

"But—" I stand in the doorway and look up at Ava, already halfway up the back hill. The word hangover has taken on rich new meaning and I'm not really feeling like moving, let alone snowshoeing up a mountain.

"Come on, Grace." Ava waves her hands above her head, gesturing me toward her. "It's gorgeous!"

By the time I strap on the old-fashioned wooden snowshoes and trudge all the way outside into the bright sun, Ava has faded into a tiny little dot moving steadily up the peak. I follow her tracks in the brilliant white hard-packed snow. I move quickly. I crunch along the mountainside.

Panting.

Sweating.

For a good five minutes the only sound is my heavy breathing and my feet breaking through the top layer of crusty ice. Every so often I get a whiff of last night's exploits, rancid alcohol mingled with salty sweat oozing out of my pores, a faithful reminder of my complete stupidity.

I stop for a second, squinting in the blinding reflection of sun and snow, and strip to my wool sweater, tying my parka around my waist.

I spot Ava up by the tree line, the start of the woods.

"Avaaa!" My voice ricochets across the acres like a pinball. "Ava, wait up." The closer I get to her the more I whine.

"Ava," I cry out. "Do I really have to go talk to someone I don't even know? I mean, why do I have to go. Why can't I just, like—"

Crunch.

Crunch.

Crunch.

My empty pleas finally come face-to-face with

Ava, sitting on a fallen log, chewing dried salmon strips.

She is unmoved.

Not impressed.

She hands me her water bottle. "Theona is an incredible person, Grace." Ava pauses to hand me some salmon. "Try it, it's good," she says, continuing her speech while I chew. "Listen, you need to give this a chance."

"But—" I sigh, I chew, I swallow.

"Ava," I start again. "There is nothing wrong with me! I just made one stupid mistake, and—"

Ava cuts me off. "Look." She's angry. "You really don't have a choice. It doesn't matter that I think it's a good idea, which I do—

"Grace, the fact is this is coming from your mom, not me."

"But there's nothing wrong with me!" I throw my poles down. "Why do I have to go to a shrink!"

Ava loads her gear back into her pack. "Theona Briggs is not a shrink, she is a therapist, a community health aide. She is the medical RN for the entire island, and she happens to be lovely, Grace, you'd be lucky to spend some time with her." Ava's eyes are bright, clear, convincing. She almost has me. "Just give her a chance—" she says.

"I just like, God! I mean, I just made one stupid

mistake, that's all. I was like, experimenting and, you know, I get the message, I get it loud and clear, okay? I'll never drink again." My voice is rising, shaking. It's not flattering, and it certainly isn't pretty. I work to lower the pitch, to sound more composed, not like a raving lunatic. "I don't see why I have to go see a total stranger and talk to her about—"

Ava cuts me off.

"Look," she says, sounding angry again. "This isn't something we are going to debate, okay? This isn't a punishment, this is something to help you, you've been through a lot and—"

Ava stops suddenly. "Look," she whispers, pointing into the forest behind me.

"Dall sheep," she says softly. "Do you see them?"

I nod.

"They come down the mountain in the winter. The snow is lower down here and they're hungry."

"Hungry?" I repeat. "Will they, like, attack us?"

"No!" Ava laughs.

"Look at the horns, aren't they magnificent?"

"What do we do?"

"Nothing," Ava whispers. "I've seen them up here a dozen times, but I never get sick of it." She shakes her head. "Gorgeous," she sighs.

I watch the herd of white cottony sheep, foraging,

searching, blending into the mountainside.

Ava rests her hand on my shoulder.

"You okay?"

"Yeah," I say softly. "I mean, no."

Here come the tears.

I lose it, for like, the trillionth time in the last twenty-four hours.

Right there on top of the mountain, beside a giant pine tree, like Little Bo Peep—sheep found and grazing in the distance. Ava straps her pack back on. Except for a few wisps, her hair is tucked under her hat. She looks radiant. Rosy cheeks, freckles, bright shiny eyes.

She pulls me into her, hugging me.

My sobs get louder, weepier, until I'm taking big gasping breaths. I can hardly breathe.

Ava holds me.

She just holds me for a long, long time.

"It's okay," she whispers.

"Ava," I sob. "I'm so sorry, I just—"

"Shh." She strokes my head, just like my mom. "Shh," she whispers.

My big wet tears soak her parka.

My nose is running.

I can't seem to stop.

But Ava—

She doesn't say let's go.

She doesn't tell me to pull myself together.

She just hugs me.

The sheep grazing in the distance.

"Everything is going to be okay," she whispers.

busted.

Theona Briggs's office is a few buildings up from Sadie's on Main Street. I have no trouble finding it. The building is old, with tall pillars in the front. It sort of looks like the White House, except it's mustardy yellow and the paint is peeling off.

I plop my bag down on the sidewalk and dig for the scrap of paper Ava gave me that has the office number on it. Out of the corner of my eye I see Fisher walking toward me, waving madly.

"Hey, Em!" she calls. She's smiling and adorable, and I suddenly feel terrible that I am so insecure, so self-conscious about my little "meeting," that I ran out of school and didn't tell her where I was going.

"Hey," I say, trying to sound casual, like I'm going to get my hair cut or pick up groceries, trying to sound however it is you sound when you are NOT going to see a therapist.

She stops in front of me. "I couldn't find you after school."

"Um, yeah, I have, like—

"I have an appointment." I blurt it out.

"An appointment?" She folds her arms over her chest. "With who?"

My hands get all sweaty under my mittens and my head heats up. I am not used to admitting that I need help.

I am used to pretending I'm perfect. Pretending I'm the got-it-all-together girl.

I stall. I stall with this dumb blank look and try desperately to think of what to say.

I'm so tired of lying about everything in my life, and maybe I can't tell her who I am, but at least I can stop being who I was.

Stop pretending I'm some teenage action hero.

Stop pretending I don't need help.

"Hellooo?" Fisher knocks playfully on my head. "Any day now."

I thrust the little scrap of paper in front of her face and watch Fisher's expression as she reads Ava's handwriting.

"You're going to the shrink?"

My face turns kind of red. "Ava's making me go."

"I see." Fisher grins. "Repercussions from your night of debauchery!"

"Something like that," I say, still embarrassed but managing a little smile back.

Fisher smiles too. "Make sure to tell her I say hi."

"Theona? You know her?"

"Know her? I've been seeing her since I was like, five?" Fisher slaps me on the back. "You think YOU have issues," she sighs. "Join the club."

theona.

Picture a dog, panting, with its tongue hanging out, and you have a nice little snapshot of my face as I slog up the rickety steps to the fourth floor. The hallway is empty, deserted, a no-man's-land. When I find the door to Theona's office I don't really know what I'm supposed to do. So I stand there for a few seconds, my fist cocked to knock, until I think I hear voices.

Not like, *in my head.*

Behind the door.

I press my ear up against the door and listen. I can't make any words out, just muted voices. *Laughing? Crying?* I pull my head away, guilty that I am eavesdropping but oddly relieved that I am not the only one in Medicine Hat in need of mental assistance. Sort of like, when you think you totally bombed your chemistry test and you walk out of the room and the girl who was sitting next to you says she thought she failed it too. You can't help but be happy. Relieved.

I strip off my jacket, my hat, my mittens, and my extra sweater. I pile my stuff on the floor and take a seat on the only chair in the hall directly across from Theona's door, next to a card table, a pile of magazines, and a fruit basket with no fruit.

I wait.

I fidget.

I think too much. *I can't believe I'm seeing a therapist!*

I'm kind of excited. Kind of anxious. I breathe in deeply and exhale loudly. I tap my foot.

I stand up, stretch, walk back and forth down the hallway. I look out the only window and wonder how exactly it works that the days get shorter and shorter here, that it can already be pitch black outside. I plop back down on the chair and pick up a dog-eared copy of *Personalities* magazine. I turn one page at time, look-ing at a world that seems all at once bizarre, and strange—a million miles away. Pictures of Britney (shop-ping in Paris), of the Olsen twins (lunch at the Four Seasons), Lindsay Lohan (clubbing in Barcelona), pictures of—

me.

Where is is is she?

Teen Tennis Sensation Ace Kincaid gives it all up for normal life. The mother of number-one ranked singles tennis player, Grace "Ace" Kincaid, backs her daughter's decision to retire from tennis. "It was too much," Dr. Lily Kincaid said. "Grace is fifteen years old. Most people might not understand why someone at the top of her game would step away, but I support her decision 100 percent. I couldn't be prouder. Somehow at a very young age, my daughter figured out there is more to life than tennis." Through her agent, Stan Brooks, Kincaid shocked the sports world by abruptly announcing her retirement before the start of the US Open.

Kincaid's 107-mile-per-hour serve, and blond cover-girl looks earned her lucrative endorsement deals (Mercedes-Benz, Lancôme, Nike, Pepsi, Tommy Girl), placing her career earnings at over $33 million.

"Grace Kincaid is a phenomenal tennis player. Beyond that, she is a fantastic young lady," said Brooks. "She has a lot to offer this world, more than just tennis." Current number-two singles champion, Olga Kovalenko, suddenly finds herself without one of her biggest rivals. "I have no idea where she is, and no comment. I need to focus on the Australian [Open]." Kovalenko is recovering from an ACL tear to her right knee and is expected to be out for another ten to twelve weeks. Kincaid's longtime coach, Heinz Roulph, is at peace with the move. "Sure, I'd love her to defend Wimbledon. When and if she's ready, she has my number. For now, let her be." Just where Ace is hiding is the million-dollar question. Her mother and her agent were tight-lipped on details. "I will say she is living comfortably, safely, someplace in the world," Brooks said. "We should all give her that freedom." Not everyone agrees. "The first paparazzo to get the shot is going to be a wealthy man," said celebrity photographer George James. The photo could earn someone a cool $120,000. James, famous for his aggressive celebrity stalking, is on the case. "I have leads right now in Florida, Hawaii, and eastern Oregon. We'll see."

By Jessie T. Wright
(JTW@personalitiesmag.com)

Rahib Rashad and Rebecca Davidson contributed to this story.

I quietly rip the page out of the magazine, fold it up neatly, and wedge it behind my book at the bottom of my backpack.

I will carry it like a badge.

Proof I'm here.

Proof I've changed.

Just in case I need reminding.

two minutes later.

When the door to Theona's office abruptly swings open, my surprise is met by the eyes of an old man with a bad limp and sun-stained skin. He smiles at me as if we are in the same messed-up club. I nod and watch him shuffle down the hall. I listen to his tentative steps, the creaking stairs, until it hits me.

I'm next.

Next.

My heart begins to speed up, like it does when the teacher is about to call on you. Of course, this is precisely when I hear my name.

My real name.

"Grace?"

A goddesslike-retired-surfer-mermaid type with a tangle of untamed straw-blond hair, cowgirl boots, jeans, and a tight white T-shirt that says *How about never—is never good for you?* is standing in the open doorway. She has a magnetic smile and fiery eyes. Wise eyes that I wouldn't normally notice, except hers are an out-of-this-world electric blue.

"Come on in," she says, a glint of magic in her smile.

She seems smart and feisty and very much alive.

Her eyes, her grin, revive me. I jump up out of the folding chair, grab my stuff, and walk through the open door.

inside.

The walls are covered with photographs. Kids, babies, smiling faces—postcards, hundreds of them, from far-away places.

"Have a seat," she tells me, sitting down herself in a tattered armchair placed strategically in front of a pre-historic couch with a half dozen pillows piled on top.

I park my bony butt on the very edge of the couch, careful not to make myself too comfortable, as if sitting back and settling in would be acknowledging the reality of this situation.

That I am here.

That I am doing this.

That I need help.

We look at each other.

It's awkward at first.

Like the way you feel on a plane, or a bus, when there is someone sitting right next to you and you feel like you have to say *something*. You have to fill the silence.

We do the smile thing.

I do the sigh thing.

I do the shy-little-girl thing. In my mind I berate myself. I attempt to cajole myself to speak, to not be such a baby.

All the while, Hawaii's 1972 Big Surf Champion (according to the certificate on the wall) is perfectly content. She looks at me with poise, with elegance, like a high priestess sitting on her throne.

"So," she finally speaks first. "Before we get started, I want to assure you, everything we talk about here is completely confidential."

I nod.

I exhale.

I think I smile.

"I can either call you Emily, or I can call you Grace, a beautiful name, a strong name." She smiles. "Which would you prefer?"

"Grace," I say. Ava had already told me Theona knew, but I'm still relieved all over again there is one less person I have to keep this secret with.

"Your mom and Ava have filled me in on the recent excitement in your life."

I shrug.

I nod.

I bite my bottom lip.

For a one-thousandth of a second I consider standing up, saying this was a big mistake, saying I don't really need to be here.

But I do.

I do need to be here.

I look everywhere in the room but straight ahead of me.

I look around at the postcards.

The pictures.

The richly colored fabrics on the wall.

I study the map in the corner, with its little push-pins indicating visits, or holidays, or maybe just dreams.

I do this until there is no place else for me to look, and finally turn back to her.

She is peacefully composed, her eyes smiling gently, urging me on. Maybe she's a genie or some type of Surf Voodoo Goddess, because after a few moments the awkward silence dissipates, evaporates, completely fades away.

And I finally slump back against the soft silky pillows, all at once overwhelmed, subdued. Surrendering to the quiet sensation that this is it. This is my mark. The stillness that happens before one unfolds.

Before I come undone.

one hour later.

I use an entire box of Kleenex.

I'm not kidding.

I cover every issue.

Everything!

My dad.

My mom.

Tennis.

Fear.

Guilt.

Drinking.

Running away from Tattoo Guy, from my life. By the time I get to the happier, hopeful, joyful subject of my love life, I want to lunge across the couch, grab the little clock ticking loudly on the table, and turn it back.

I want more time.

Like everyone else on this crazy island, Theona is generous with her hugs. She keeps her hand resting lightly on my back as I zip up my parka and tug my hat back on.

"Grace, the more you can let go of the sadness, the more room there will be for light." She arches her eyebrows as if she knows something is in store for me. "The more room there will be for love," she says.

"Wait. Can you like, run that by me one more time?" I ask. My eyes dart around the room. "Do you have something I can write with?"

She smiles. "You don't need to write this down, you know this already."

"I do?"

"All the love around you, it wants to come in." She smiles.

"It just needs some space, and to heal, you have to open to the sadness, to grief. Let yourself feel in order to let it go."

Um.

Whoa.

I stand there for a second and try to remember every word. As if this is a recipe, my recipe to feel better. To feel. I want to say thank you, I want to do something that will show my appreciation, my gratefulness.

I am out of words.

I'm also out of time.

"See you Friday," she tells me, one hand already turning the doorknob.

"Friday," I repeat. "And thanks," I say softly.

"You are welcome." Her voice sounds full of hope.

Hope for me.

Outside the door there is a frail wisp of a girl who I recognize from school, waiting, in my former spot. She jumps up when the door opens. The two of us scrape by each other in the hallway. I pass on the old man's knowing smile, looking into her eyes, sending love— suddenly feeling oddly lucky to be in this strange new club.

after.

I walk down the fourth-floor hallway, exhausted but buoyant in a way I didn't expect. My *after* is way better than my *before*. And as I descend the stairs to the street, I have a brazenly bold spring in my step, a straightness to my gait. I literally feel lighter, stronger, like I purged the bad stuff and left some of it balled up in my snotty wet tissues in the wicker wastebasket next to Theona's couch.

I skip the last three steps.

I take one big leap.

I land, square, balanced—

Flat on my feet.

Outside, Fisher is waiting, freezing her butt off on the front step of the building.

"Hey!" she says, springing up, the captain of my own private cheerleading squad. She slings one arm around me as we walk toward Sadie's. "How was it? Did

you like, bawl your eyes out? I always bawl my eyes out."
We giggle like sisters as we trudge through the snow.
And when Fisher and I come out from the dark cold into
the warm glow of Sadie's, I am the recipient of welcom-
ing how-do-you-do smiles that Fisher usually garners
wherever she goes. And as I wait with Fisher at the
counter for our hot cocoa and Sadie's famous just-out-of-
the-oven muffins, I think of what Theona told me. That
thing about letting the sadness flow out in order to make
room for the light.

I see it in the eyes smiling back at me.

Let the sadness flow out, to make room for the light.

Theona knows what she's doing.

She's right.

love.

Please, people! I was not born yesterday. You don't think
I'm going to waste my new effervescence, my captivating
bubbly zest. No way! I need to find my Boy Wonder. I
need to—as Fisher likes to say—*share the love.*

Sadie's is crowded, so I stand on my tippy toes and
scour the room for Teague until Fisher jabs her elbow in
my gut and nods toward the door.

"Ehhh-hem!" she says.

{Insert harp music, orchestra, gooey love song . . .}

Teague.

"Three is a crowd, baby," says Fisher with a big exaggerated wink. "I'm out of here." She lowers her voice and wiggles her eyebrows. "Your *lover boy* can take you home."

"Fisher, that's ridiculous, come on!" I grab her hand.
I pull her back to me.

"No. Really." She puts on her hat, zips up her parka, and kisses my cheek like the French do, both sides. "Let the lo-o-o-ove in!" she croons.

let love in.

I don't know what has come over me.

All I can say is that this crying thing, the purging thing, the get-the-sadness-out thing. IT WORKS!

I sashay, sway, glide toward Teague.

I don't even recognize my walk.

"Hey!" I say, beaming.

Teague's eyes light up. "Hey!" he answers, looking up from his homework.

I help myself to a seat.

I feel like I'm under some sort of confidence spell.

Teague smiles back at me as he nods toward Fisher skipping out the door. "What sort of mischief has my cousin dragged you into?"

"Nothing!" I blush.

"Riiight," says Teague, tapping me on the end of my nose with his pencil.

Gulp.

"Hey, so how was this weekend? I couldn't really make it to the—"

I put up my hand. "Don't even ask," I say, stopping him before he brings it up. The party.

"Yeah, well." Teague shakes his head. "I had a feeling that was going to be a bust. I heard that a bunch of guys from Hawkshead were up. Their village is dry, so they always come here to drink and buy alcohol and smuggle it back. Bunch of gas huffers."

"Gas huffers?"

Teague shakes his head. "You don't even want to know."

"So." I smile this flirty smile at Teague and try to think of a different subject. Quick.

Teague just—

Well, he moves closer to me, his face. Really close.

I turn completely red. *Completely.*

"What's got into you?" he asks. "Your eyes are all rosy."

I shrug.

"The truth," I say, arching my eyebrows. "The truth has set me free."

God! Where am I getting this stuff!

"Hmmm, mysterious." Teague looks into my eyes and moves a smidgen closer.

Okay, I'm swooning.

Swooning.

I can't believe this is even happening to me.

"So, um—" I start.

Teague smiles.

He lets me squirm.

"Um, how's your job?" I blurt out. "I mean, jobs."

Teague shrugs. "Pays the bills." I immediately want to take back my question because when I bring up work he sits back in his chair, he pulls away.

I scrunch up my nose. "You have to pay your own bills?"

"Well, yeah, I mean, who else will do it, you know? Plus, I'm saving for college, and for a new snowmobile, and a few other materialistic things that I definitely don't need, but—" He breaks into a smile. "I kind of want."

The air comes back into my lungs, along with the uncomfortable reality of my gazillions of way-too-much money. The sudden memory of my other life.

Of who I really am.

Teague notices. "You okay?" he asks.

And I feel his hand.

Under the table.

On my knee.

Oh. MyGod.

"Yeah, umm," I stammer.

He smiles.

His hand doesn't move.

It's warm and strong, and—

Who would know a knee was so sensitive!

"Umm." I blush. I look into his eyes, his crazy-bright eyes.

I look at him, not quite believing how you can wake up and think you are having the worst week of your life and then, *bam!*

It turns out to be the best.

dusk.

Teague drives me home on his beat-up old snow-mobile—held together by a thread. Literally. Threadlike frayed rope and duct tape, a lot of duct tape, but it works. And he doesn't drive too fast. He is careful with his cargo, careful with me.

Of course, with my newly minted courage and the room I've made for love, I hold on anyway. I boldly wrap my arms around him and rest my head on his shoulder,

and together we negotiate the winding back roads, synchronized like a team as we lean right, then left, around
the curves. One simple gesture under the table at Sadie's
and the wall has crumbled. That unspoken boundary that
separates friends from more than friends—it's down.

Officially lowered.

Bulldozed.

Touching is encouraged, sanctioned. I can't stop.

SO.

We get to the top of the driveway and get off the snowmobile. Bear bolts out of the darkness to greet us.

"Hey, boy," says Teague, scratching back Bear's ears.

"Yes, nice to see you too." He nestles his nose to
Bear's, giving him an Eskimo kiss, which is funny,
because, well, Teague *is* an Eskimo.

I take off my helmet and shake out my matted-down
hair, which feels longer and suddenly sexier than I
remembered it to be.

We stand there, Bear panting at our feet.

"So, um, thanks!" I say, half wanting to invite him
in but half knowing I should let him go. It's dark. It's a
school night. I should say good-bye while everything is
perfect.

Say good-bye before the spell breaks.

I begin to step back, toward the cabin but—

"Wait a sec," he says, setting his hand on my shoulder.

When he touches me. *God.*

"I want to ask you something," he says.

"Ask away."

"Well, what I want to ask you is—" Teague kneels down to attend to Bear. "Yes, boy, you just wait one second," he says, ruffling his ears.

He stands back up.

"Okay, so," he starts again.

I smile.

A big silly grin.

This boy is so cute, seriously, I—

"What I wanted to ask you is—"

He takes off his gloves and wraps his somehow warm hands around my mittens. *Honestly, I think I'm going to die.*

"What I want to ask you is, two days before Christmas, there is a big winter festival at the harbor." He pauses for a second and squeezes my hands.

His dimples are in full working order.

"It's kind of a boy-ask-girl thing, and I was wondering if you, Ms. Emily O'Brien, would like to go?"

"Like, together?" I blurt out. *Oh my God, did I just say that!*

"Yeah." Teague grins. "That would be the idea." He puts his bare hands into my mittens, our first official hand-holding moment, and I don't just feel it in my hands. "There's ceremonial dancing, tons of food, a band up from Juneau, and—"

I put my bare finger up to his lips.

I have no idea where I get this move.

"Shhhhh," I say.

For a second we stand in the dark moonlight with Bear resting beneath us.

"Teague Denali." I smile at him. "The answer is yes."

walking on air.

I run. No, I float. I float up the hill and burst into the front door of the cabin. I strip off my parka, my boots, my sweater, and throw down my backpack.

"Ava?"

"Hellooo?" I call.

"I'm ho-o-o-ome!" I sing.

It's kind of weird because the woodstove is blazing hot, there are candles all over the place, and music is playing. Wait, the table's set—

For three.

part four

"Grief can take care of itself,
but to get the full value of joy
you must have somebody to divide it with."

—Mark Twain

steamy.

Walking into the cabin is like walking into the page of a romance novel. There are clothes scattered on the floor, strewn about like they were peeled off in a spur-of-the-moment moment, if you know what I mean. And as I walk through the cabin calling Ava's name, it occurs to me that Ava might have her own little somethin'-somethin' brewing. Maybe it's the guy she talked about in the truck? The bush pilot? Maybe it's the guy who drops off the wood?

I'm giddy and jumpy and still high from my own steamy, soap-opera moment.

"Ava?"

"Hello-o-o-o?"

The kitchen is a mess. Two wineglasses sit almost empty on the counter, the cutting board is out, onions chopped, mushrooms diced. I peek into the pot sitting on a hot plate.

Steamed rice.

Salmon.

Greens.

"Ava?" I call again.

Bear joins me.

"That's right, boy," I say, relieved to have him by my side as I open the back door and step into the darkness.

"Ava?"

suprise.

I practically smack into her. Ava. Naked. Well, not totally: she's wrapped up in a flimsy white hotel towel. Ava and—

My jaw just about drops off my face.

"Aloha!" Big T emerges from the cold, with nothing on but a towel wrapped tightly around his waist, like a football lineman walking around the locker room. My face lights up, my eyes pop out. "Oh-my-gosh! What are you doing here—" I go to hug him.

"Hold that thought," he says, blushing, one hand clutching his towel and the other gathering his assorted garments from the living-room floor. "One sec," he says, winking at me and hightailing it across the cabin to the safe confines of the bathroom.

I look toward Ava, still standing in her towel, with this silly, glowing kind of flighty look that I have not seen on her face before and it hits me—

Duuuhhh, Grace. "Wait." I smile. "Are you two, like—"

Ava jumps in before I can finish. "No!" she says in a voice that is not entirely convincing. "Grace, Tobias is here because—"

"Tobias?" I repeat and kind of giggle. I have never heard anyone use Big T's given name. Tobias.

I smile at Ava. I'm on to her.

Ava rolls her eyes. She is blushing, big time. "As I was saying—" She clears her throat.

Her freckles glisten, still wet from the—*Wait, what were they doing out there, anyhow?*

"Grace." Ava smiles. "This isn't how it seems."

I lift an eyebrow and smirk.

"Really," she says, collecting her own clothes from the floor. "Actually, Tobias came in early this morning after you left for school. I picked him up at the ferry, and—"

She is absolutely gleaming.

"What?" Ava stops midsentence.

"Nothing," I say, smiling back.

"Anyway!" Ava steps into her jeans. "The good news is, he helped me haul, hook up, and fill our brand spankin' new, tricked-out, custom-built—" She pauses, drawing out the suspense.

"Yes?" I take the bait.

Ava pulls on her T-shirt and speaks as her head bursts through the top. "Hot tub!"

"Hot tub!" I squeal and jump up and down. "For real?"

"Yep!"

"You mean, with like, HOT water?"

"Hot water," says Ava. "It's heated by an underwater stove. You feed it wood so you don't have to keep the water warm all the time. I first used one when I was in Japan—they are quite clever, and—" She pauses and raises her eyebrows. "What!"

Her face is about as bright as the candles flickering on the table. She is honestly too beautiful for words.

"Nothing," I repeat, beaming back at her.

Ava pulls her sweater over her head and brushes her hair back, all the while talking with a hair tie in the clutches of her front teeth. "We spent all day getting that bad girl up and running." Ava removes the hair thingie and ties her hair back in a neat ponytail. "It's paradise, under the stars, soaking in hot water, I can't wait for you to try it—"

"Definitely!" I say. "Wait—" I scrunch up my face. "What's the bad news?"

Just then, T comes out of the bathroom, wearing jeans and a button-up shirt. He's lost weight—he looks great, different. The three of us sit down at the table.

"Okay, so here's the deal," starts Ava, her voice suddenly heavier than before.

I brace myself, crossing my arms over my chest, breathing in deep.

"Your mom and Mariko are a little concerned about some recent inquiries. Apparently someone hacked into your mom's cell phone account in L.A. and—"

I wilt.

My heart sinks.

I can't even swallow.

Ava reaches out across the table and covers my hand with hers. "Grace, hold on—it's not that bad," she tells me. "The thing is, my cell is a California number, so nobody can possibly know where you are just yet, but we think the paparazzi might have my name. Some folks have been snooping around, asking questions."

I slump further into my seat.

I can't believe this. Just when everything was going so—

Ava squeezes my hand. "Look, you don't have to leave, at least, not yet."

"I don't?" My eyes widen. I sound like I'm ten.

T jumps in. "That's why I'm here." He winks.

I love T.

Ava smiles. "We just need to be super careful, and—"

"Wait, I totally get to stay?"

"Totally," they say.

before dinner.

I throw my boots on and head outside in the moonlight. I sink through the deep soft snow as I trek across the backyard to the back of the shed where I keep the stacked dry wood. "Hello?" I sing. "Hello-o-o?" I say, addressing any lurking brown bears waiting in the shadows. "Don't eat me, okay? I like it here. I want to stay."

I pile a half dozen logs into my arms, stacking them so high that I have to peer over the wood as I retrace my sunken steps back to the cabin. Inside, I brush off the snow, the wood chips, the dirt clinging to the front of my sweater, and kneel by the woodstove, distributing the logs until the fire is blazing, popping, shooting red-orange streaks up the chimney.

"Nice," I say, talking to the leaping orange flames.

I listen to the fire crackle, the music in the background, the budding romance in the kitchen. I fall back on the couch and stretch out, cradling my head in my hands like I'm doing sit-ups. *Sit-ups!*

I smile.

I don't miss them one bit.

dinner.

The three of us sit around the table.

We say grace, we dive in.

"Wait!" I look at T, my mouth still full. "Where are you staying?"

"Yes," says Ava, her eyes twinkling. "Where *are* you staying?"

I think they're teasing me. They're like two teenagers and I'm the mom. T waits until he's finished chewing. "I'm staying at a lodge down the road. It used to be—"

"Oh, right," I cut him off. "With the blue metal roof?"

"Exactly," he says.

"Whose is it?" I ask, shoveling in more stew.

Ava glances at T. The two lovebirds are already communicating in some sort of silent code.

T starts. "Well, it's a friend of Ava's, and he—"

"Doesn't use it anymore," Ava jumps in.

Ava looks out the window at the snow. "We're going

to have ourselves a blizzard tonight. The driving is going to be—"

"Risky?" says T.

I know for a fact Ava's snowmobile will work just fine. "What about the—" *Duuhhh, Grace.* I gulp back my words.

"What about the what?" Asks Ava.

"Nothing." I grin.

I am so on to them.

Ava is not a good actress. "Hey!" Her face lights up like she just had a sudden inspiration. "Why don't you stay here tonight?"

T smiles. "Sure, I guess I could just sleep on the floor in here, by the fire."

Ava jumps up to clear the plates. "It's settled, then!" she says, floating into the kitchen.

Sadness out.

Love in.

december.

My days are edible. A dream. For the first time since I quit playing tennis, there is flow. Perfect flow. I feel it again.

I knit, I sew, I learn to drive a snowmobile and run over T's toe. When I go to see Theona, I walk fast—on a sojourn, a mission. I would never have guessed how good it feels to have someone totally and completely listen. And so I spring up the four flights to the Surf Goddess Supreme. The rickety steps are familiar—I know which ones creak. The smoothness of the wood greets my feet. Some days I walk down the hallway actually whistling a tune. I nod at my special secret friends. I send well wishes, my eyes wide like the moon. My quiet smile says, *I'm okay? You okay? Great! See you soon.*

At the end of my hour-long sessions, Theona always pitches me geniuslike gems. I diligently write them down on little pieces of paper that I keep by my bed. *Feel your power, be okay with saying no, the less you keep it bottled up, the more room for better things to grow.*

Sometimes she has me hit a pillow, which was incredibly strange at first, to punch and think of what I want, what I need, or what I wish I could really say, but don't. Feel your power, Grace! I think, as tiny down feathers burst out of the seams like good-luck confetti celebrating my dreams.

Fisher and I recite Theona verbatim, like scholars. Affirmations and sayings tucked in our pockets like silver dollars. At the bowling alley, decked out in my pink retro shirt, I am in full-goddess mode. "I deserve to have boundaries!" I announce, giggling and hurling the ball down the lane. The pins crash and tumble, and I twirl around. "And I need to—" I pause, rolling my eyes back into my head, scouring the messy filing cabinet in the back of my brain. "Oh, I've got it!" I flop into the seat at the scorer's table next to Fisher. "Theona says I need to like, let go of wanting to control whether someone approves of me or loves me, and like—"

"Hey! She told me that too!"

"Well, I love you," I say.

Fisher hurls the ball and looks back over her shoulder before the pins fall.

"Well, thanks, Emmy Lou," she says.

"I love you too."

the shortest day.

On the shortest day, the winter solstice, I watch the sun set at 3:03 P.M. from inside our classroom. We "ooh" and "aah," like little kids watching fireworks on the Fourth of July. I press my nose against the window and drink in the purple northern lights, the last lingering bit of shimmering sky.

At home, before the festival—

Yes, that festival! I prepare myself like an Egyptian queen. I fire up the underwater woodstove and soak in the tub for an eternity under the stars. As I step out of the wooden barrel, steam comes off my skin and I dash through the snow, in that space between pain and delight. I feel the magic of this place as my feet crunch down on the ice.

Inside, the cabin is warm and bright and cozy, and I run, wrapped in my towel, past Ava and T reading on the couch. I scurry straight into the bathroom, where I lay my towel on the floor and hunker down by the heat vent piping in warm air from the stove. I look back at my reflection, at my emerging honey blond roots. I stay on my towel like a girl at the beach and go to town with Ava's essential oils, dumping half a bottle of her lavender potion into the palm of my hand and massaging it into my legs, my arms—I even put some on my neck, under my chin. When I'm done I feel like a snake.

I've shed my skin.

I surface from the bathroom smelling like a bouquet of freshly picked lavender. My lips slathered with Ava's homemade rose petal balm, my hair silky soft, I slink through the living room, a long white towel wrapped around the length of my body, another wrapped like a turban around my head.

"Someone's smellin' puuurty!" teases Ava, smiling at me.

T raises an eyebrow. "Hmmm, maybe we should tag along."

"No!" I snap, looking back at them from the ladder to my loft. "I mean, no, I'm good," I try again, this time smiling sweetly.

Ava winks up at me. "She'll be so fine," she says, nudging T with her elbow. "She can do it. This is her day."

I get dressed in my loft. It feels like I'm getting ready for the prom, except the party is outside, it's twenty degrees, and the decorations—the mountains, the sea, the boats in the harbor—they're real. No tenth-grade committee has to make them. I comb out my hair and put in two barrettes, the way Ava sometimes wears hers. In lieu of a long fussy prom dress, I pile on layers and layers of clothes. Long underwear, my favorite boiled-wool sweater, and jeans.

While I wait for Teague to arrive, I sit on the floor and slither into my snow pants, the legs of which scrape together when I walk, loudly trumpeting every move I make. I pull my parka on, my big furry hat, and catch a glimpse of my formal attire in the mirror. Wisps of red hair peeking out from under my hat. I look genuinely happy.

I tilt my head sideways and smile back.

thirty minutes later.

I wait outside, with Bear, at the top of the hill by the cabin. I sit on a patch of hardened ice and listen for the familiar sound of Teague's rumbling snowmobile muffler. I wait. And wait. I wait so long I start to talk to Bear.

"Where is he?" I take several long sighs and throw pieces of ice into the forest. "Teague?" I say into the night. "Where are you?"

"Have I been stood up?" I hold my hand on Bear's velvet coat, hugging him close to me. "Bear," I whisper. "Did he love me and leave me?" I ask.

"Are we through?"

yes.

I have been officially stood up. Ava comes out with no jacket, her boots, and the blanket from the couch wrapped around her like a shawl. "Still not here?"

"I wish he had a phone," I say. "I wish I could call. What if he—"

Ava throws half the blanket over my shoulders.

"Why don't you take my Honda out and go pick

him up. T and I will come down to the harbor later in the truck."

My eyes pop out. "By myself?"

"Sure." She shrugs.

I'm starting to shiver.

"Just be sure to stay on the main road into town, and watch out for critters jumping out from the woods."

I nod.

"Wait, do you know where Teague lives?"

"Oh." I roll my eyes. "Good point!"

"It's the apartment over Sadie's. If you are standing in front of Sadie's, the entrance is on the left, red door."

"Over Sadie's, red door," I repeat, my teeth chattering.

Ava opens her hand to reveal her keys.

"The helmet is in the shed next to the—"

"I know!" I shout back over my shoulder, already bounding down the icy white hill.

crazy.

I stand on my feet, Fisher-style, and ride the Honda into town like I'm taming a bucking bronco. I am gutsy, in control, happy to for once be the rescuer—not the rescue-e.

By the harbor, Main Street is completely blocked off

with yellow policelike barriers. The street is overflowing with people, smiling, dancing in the middle of the road.

Everyone in Medicine Hat must be here.

I park where the man with the flashlights directs me, leave my helmet, and walk past a raging bonfire spitting sky-high flames, past ceremonial dancers in handmade parkas, children playing all sorts of games, until finally, I'm standing in front of Sadie's, and I open the red door.

At the top of the stairs there is only one door. It doesn't have a wreath or anything. It doesn't even say whose door it is, but I'm pretty sure this is it.

I knock. I wait. My heart is beating out of my chest. "Teague?" I call. "Hellooo?"

There is no response.

The stairwell smells like someone spilled gasoline.

I plug my nose. I try again. This time I take off my glove and pound harder. "Hellooo?" I repeat. "Teague?"

I can hear a television.

Weird.

"Hello?" I try one more time.

I am about to give up, turn around, try and devise a plan B, when I hear footsteps.

So I step back.

I fidget with my hair.

I prepare to smile.

To look cute.

But when the door flies open—

I can't believe who I see.

huh?

Tattoo Guy.

In the flesh.

Like, literally.

Jeans. No shirt.

Jesus Christ tattooed across his bare white chest in dark gothic letters. His pants hang gangster-style, clinging to his bony hips.

"Um, hey," I say, confused. "Is this Teague's house?"

"Maybe," he answers. His face is blank, vague, void of emotion.

Maybe?

His eyes light up. "Don't I like, know you from someplace?"

"No," I lie. "Do you know where he is? Teague, I mean."

Tattoo Guy scowls. "Do I look like my brother's keeper?"

Brother?

Huh?

His face contorts into that same twisted smile I

remember from the party, and it occurs to me that maybe I should leave. *Like, immediately.*

He calls after me. "By the way, name's Abe." He pauses, just long enough for me to feel his eyes on my back. "I'm older, older and better, if you want to try me."

Focus on the door, Grace.

Keep walking, Grace.

And you know, I'm almost there, I almost make it, my hand is on the knob when—

He yells down to me.

"Whatever, bitch."

Bitch?

Maybe this should come with one of those warnings, like, with ginsu knives, you know, *Do not try this at home.* But I turn around and glare back at this guy with a strength I didn't even know I owned. "Look," I say. "It may come as a surprise to you, but I don't appreciate being called a bitch. I have a name, okay? It's *Grace.* Use it. And for your information, I am looking for Teague because I think he may have gotten in an accident, as in he may be hurt, okay? So like, you can either help me find him or—"

"Yo chill," he says, suddenly looking like a scared little boy. "Whatever." He shrugs. "He might have said something about heading up to Ava Grady's, and hey, I was just having fun with you—"

Blah, blah, blah, blah.

News flash.

I'm already out the door.

fast.

I tear down Main Street like a gazelle. My legs are long, powerful, a god-given extra gear. I am drunk with my own power, my resilience, my newfound strength. I run like I have a cape sweeping behind me, moving effortlessly through the crowds, through fire-lit spaces. The wind blusters and bites at my face, so I accelerate, I pick up the pace. And I begin to notice people noticing me, cheering, waving, stepping out of my way. At the end of Main Street, the crowd begins to part—people stand and clap and shout. I am adept, skilled, trained for speed. And sure, yes, I will admit it—I enjoy the attention, I enjoy the fact that they sense my proficiency. Maybe being appreciated is some sort of human need.

I get to the parking lot, and straddle the Honda and gas the clutch, past the man directing traffic, past a gazillion pickup trucks. Finally I turn up back onto the open road, I blast up the hill toward the Lookout. I am emboldened with a charge. I am a one-person emergency team, my eyes combing the roads, the ditches. Probing the never-ending darkness for Teague.

he's alive.

When I spot Teague's silhouette, standing in his fur parka and wolverine hat, I actually let out a gasp. His broken-down Honda is pulled off the side of the road, unbelievably close to where I first met him, a trillion days ago, on my bike, in the ditch.

I must have flown right by him on my way to town.

I pull the snowmobile up to him like it's a limousine, but instead of pressing a button and lowering the fancy tinted window, I just push up the face shield on my helmet.

My eyes water from the cold.

"Hey, sailor," I say, returning his mile-wide-hallelujah grin. "Need a lift?"

five minutes later.

On one of the longest, darkest, quite possibly coldest day of the year, the harbor is lit up like a summer carnival, with hundreds of festive lanterns strung on ropes above the docks. Women dressed in gorgeous muskrat parkas busily preparing caribou, smoked seal, walrus flippers, and carving a massive slab of celebratory whale blubber. Little children bundled up in buttery-soft sealskin suits with lush fur lining scampering about, squealing with joy, with laughter. It's magical and alive, and I physically pause before stepping onto the dock to try to take it all in.

To remember.

The pier is lined with flaming torches, an offering to rekindle the sleeping sun. Every few steps Teague's shoulder brushes against mine and sparks fly that I think could wake anything or anyone. We walk like this, touching, but not, spiraling into some sort of alternate love universe, stopping to admire exhibits of intricate ivory carvings, handwoven baskets, animal-skin blankets. We walk and we walk, ambling blissfully down the dock, until if we walk any farther we would drop right off.

On the last chunk of the wooden pier, the same spot where I first stepped off the ferry, Teague and I slip into a large crowd gathered around some kind of elaborate drumming ceremony. Native men, clad in robes and masks, pounding on barrels sheathed with sealskin. Their hand movements are synchronized perfectly. It's beautiful. I watch, completely mesmerized, until Teague wraps his fingers around mine, which normally would be, well, perfect, except I am not normal and I'm far from perfect. I panic. The type of panic the universe kindly bestows upon you when the very thing you want to happen *happens*. For a brief second I consider the obvious solution of letting his hand go. But that would leave me with short-term comfort and long-term misery.

So—

I stick with it.

I settle into the closeness, the unease.

I close my eyes.

I breathe.

The drumming becomes dreamlike, hypnotic, I get lost in the colors, the music, the repetitive looping rhythmic beat. It's enchanting and elegant, and for a second, standing there attached to Teague, I am certain the drumming is not just awakening the sun. It's awakening me.

At the end of the ceremony the crowd erupts in applause and Teague leans into me, still holding my hand. "I want you to meet someone," he tells me. I follow him as he steps into some sort of line that has spontaneously formed behind one of the drummers. I watch as people bow before him like he is some sort of prophet.

"What are they doing?" I whisper.

"It's a tradition." He smiles quietly. "A way to show respect for elders."

When it's our turn, the two of us step in front of the man, our hands linked, as if we are bride and groom standing before a minister. I don't know who this guy is, but I have butterflies. Teague bows. So I do too.

For the first time since that day in Sadie's, Teague says something in his native language, then turns to me.

"Emily, this is my grandfather," he says proudly. "Cal Denali." The old man removes his colorful mask.

I know the smile.

My friend from Theona's.

He reaches out and takes my hand in his and holds it for a very long while. He doesn't say anything about Theona's or, well, anything. His hand is warm and soft and strong for an old man. I feel like he is some sort of shaman, blessing me. And it doesn't feel weird—it feels just the way my life is supposed to be.

dance.

In the parking lot by the docks, under an enormous tent warmed by the shine of the bonfire, there is an all-out hoedown, minus the overalls, the hay, and the pig roast. All of Medicine Hat is here. Fisher, snuggled up to Elliot (one of Teague's very cute friends), Sadie, Theona, migrant workers, hippies, natives, whites, familiar friendly faces, all steeped in trancelike harmony, eyes closed, arms flailing, beckoning the return of light.

Teague turns to me, his eyes wide as if to say, *Let's go!*

Why not! I shrug, and smile and tie my bulky parka around my waist, tuck my gloves into the sleeve, and slip my hand back around Teague's, pinching myself that his hand is actually still there, where I left it, waiting for me.

We walk onto the makeshift plywood dance floor together, weaving ourselves, our bodies, into the mayhem.

Teague is flawless. A pro.

I'm stiff as a board, and I think too much.

But my Boy Wonder is a patron saint.

He leans in close. "You're doing great!" he says, his lips brushing against my ear, thank you very much.

He twirls me.

He holds me up.

He looks into my eyes.

Yes, I think I could quite possibly just lie down and die.

I am boosted by his confidence. His spirit. The way he doesn't seem to care what other people think.

And then this miraculous thing happens.

As we dance—

I tilt my head back and soak it in.

The magic, the unfiltered joy.

I finally just—

Let go.

good night moon.

The music has slowed, my parka's still tied around my waist, my sweaty head is nestled on Teague's strapping shoulder, and I'm wondering what I possibly did in some past life to deserve such bliss, such a bounty of good fortune, when I feel a tap on the top of my head, and open my eyes to see Ava and T smiling at me.

Um, can you say, embarrassing!

I pull away from Teague and turn three shades of red.

Ava winks at me.

"Teague," she says. "This is Tobias. Tobias, Teague."

Teague and T shake and nod quietly, manly, the way guys do. "Glad to see you two made it," says T.

"Yeah." Teague squeezes my hand. "I had to be rescued." He smiles, his magnetic dark eyes still dancing with me. "But thanks to Em—"

Em. I like that.

Em,

Em,

Em.

"Hey," says Ava, "I hate to break it to you two, but—" She smiles sympathetically. "It's time to go."

My lower lip pops out in this *pleeease* type of

goggley-eyed pleading that is entirely new to me but apparently not beneath me.

"I know," says Ava. "But things are going to be ending here soon. And I'd rather you not drive, with people drinking tonight." She pauses. "I'll tell you what. Say your good-byes, Tobias is going to drive the truck, and I'm going to take you on the Honda. It's late, I think that would be—"

Teague squeezes my hand again. "I've gotta get going too. It's late, and—"

He hugs me. Tight. His arms are strong and warm and my face presses into his chest.

I shut my eyes and breathe him in.

I don't let go first.

part five

"Be my singing lesson.

Be my song.

When I tell you I'm falling,

Tell me I'm strong."

—Patty Griffin

bright.

I wake up to pink morning light streaming through the window above my bed, and squint up into the stillness while I rub my eyes and wake my head. My brain is still recalibrating, foggy, in that hard-to-reach place where I know there is something I am really happy about but I can't quite think of it yet.

Then in one beautiful gushing moment,

I remember.

I remember why I'm so deliriously happy.

I remember last night.

Teague.

{Cue music video.}

The dancing, his arms, the way he held me. *Thank*

you, God! I pull my T-shirt up over my mouth and my nose and breathe in to see if he is still on me, sniffing for proof, the fragrance of his musky-sweet scent. I grin and stretch like a cat, letting out a loud yawn, snug in my nest, this modest little futon better than any five-star hotel I have ever stayed at. Better than the best.

Home, I think. Burning wood, breakfast cooking. I breathe all that in too. The sunrise dripping in, the eerily quiet pink-orange hue.

And so I have this urge to share it.

Share this big expansive love.

I lean over the railing to look down from above.

And I know it.

Immediately.

Something weird is going on.

Something is not right.

downstairs.

Ava is speaking into the phone in a hushed, whispery, this-can't-be-good-news kind of tone. Her hand gestures are fast and furious, and when she hangs up, she's not just angry, she looks sad.

"Ava?" I say softly.

My stomach knotting up.

"Is everything okay?"

As soon as she looks up at me.

I know.

Her eyes say everything.

"Grace," she says. "I'm so sorry."

"But—" Tears tumble out of my eyes.

"But, what about Christmas?" I sob.

"And what about—"

I turn to T, as if he can fix this.

Who am I kidding.

The paparazzi are ruthless.

Not just ruthless—

Insane.

They will swoop down on Medicine Hat like a swarm of vultures diving for prey. They will stop at nothing, threatening, the best people, the best place—

I know.

I have no choice.

I know what I have to do.

i have to go.

I lament on the sofa, with Bear consoling me, his face nuzzled in my lap. "I know, boy," I say into his soft floppy ears. "I know." Bear's ears shoot straight up as the cabin door opens. Ava walks back in, covered from head to toe with a dusting of shimmering white snow.

"Well, I'll tell you what—nobody will be flying in tonight. T is still shoveling, I'm taking a break—" Ava takes off her coat, her hat, shakes out her long dark hair, and collapses onto the couch next to me.

"The only one flying in tonight will be Rudolph." She smiles. "Definitely no wily photographers. Trust me Grace, no plane can make it through this." She looks at me with her dazzling blue eyes. She scratches Bear's ears. "I know boy. I'm sad too," Ava sighs, and pulls me close to her.

I want to say a thousand things. I want to tell her how much I adore her. More than I thought it was possible to love someone who is not your mom, or a boy, or related to you. I want to thank her. I want to thank her a thousand times, a thousand times and more—

"Oh, Grace," she says.

And just at that moment, the fire lets out a crackling snap, and I lurch my head back and smack my skull against Ava's tooth. "Ow!" I yelp, and feel my head for blood. Out of the corner of my eye I see Ava holding her mouth.

We both lose it.

Laughing.

I laugh until my ribs ache, and I fall back, soothed by the warmth of the fire.

I don't have to speak.

I don't have to say anything.

The silence is easy.

Peaceful.

Someplace along the way, I stopped having to try.

fish bowl.

I find Fisher at the bowling alley, dressed in her pink bowling shirt, her wild thick black hair swooped up in some type of bird's-nest-meets-knitting-needle bun.

When she sees me she takes a running leap and hugs me so hard she almost knocks me off my feet.

"Start talking!" she teases. "And don't go leaving out any details!"

I slip off my boots.

I lace up my size-ten funky bowling shoes.

I smile at Fisher.

"So what's up with Ell-i-ot?" I dish it right back.

Her face turns bright red and her eyes get all googly. I've never seen Fisher like this.

"Hmm, can you elaborate on that?" I pick out my favorite marbled purple bowling ball from the rack.

"He's just—" She shrugs. "I don't know, he's like the first guy who actually asks me about me and doesn't like, drone on and on and on about himself."

"Sounds sweet." I smile, I nod, I try to figure out

how I'm going to tell her about—*leaving*. "Listen, um, Fisher, I—" I start, but Fisher cuts me off.

"Save it," she says, springing out of her seat. "Please! I'd have to be blind to not know you are in love, in luuuuv," she sings.

I blush.

I bowl.

I sit back down next to Fisher at the scorer's table.

I look into her eyes.

I really need to tell her. I'm running out of time.

"Look, Fisher, I have to tell you something, and—"

"Wait, is this some ploy to beat me?" Fisher cackles, the holiday crowd looks over toward us.

"You cannot trick a trickster!" Fisher jumps up and waits for the ball I just used to shoot up that ball-returner contraption.

And it occurs to me.

I think she knows.

Not about who I am—

That I'm leaving.

She knows what I have to tell her.

Only, she doesn't want me to say it.

She doesn't want me to go.

finally.

On the stone wall, with snow dumping a mile a minute, out of a dark blustering sky. I tell her that I have to go back to California. That I'm leaving.

"What?" says Fisher. "Like, when?"

"Tomorrow," I answer.

"Well, that sucks!" Fisher breaks off a long sharp icicle and hurls it off the cliff, crashing toward the sea.

First she tries to make a joke about it.

"Sure, go hang out with the movie stars," she says, heaving another icicle off the ridge. "Go and leave me for the beautiful people, the sunshine, the beaches. Sure, real cool, Em."

Then she gets all serious.

She stops talking.

She keeps throwing ice off the cliff.

She's pissed.

"Malibu isn't all that great, Fisher," I tell her. "I mean, actually, I think you are the lucky one. I would rather stay here."

"What!" She makes a face. "I would give anything to be you, to live in California. I would like, maybe I'll try out for *American Idol* or something and—"

"But, um, you don't sing, do you?"

"Okay, maybe not *American Idol*." She rolls her eyes. "But someday I'm going to be famous. I'll learn to play guitar—I'll be a famous rock star."

"Hmmm." I smile at her. "You would be an awesome rock star." I elbow her in the gut. "I mean, you do have the rock star look going, and the rock star boyfriend, but—"

I toss a snowball and watch it fall. "I don't know if you would want to be famous."

Fisher looks at me like I'm crazy.

She laughs. "Who in their right mind wouldn't want to be famous? All that money? I wouldn't have to worry about anything." Her eyes drift off. "I would have a tricked-out car, and a big house like the ones on MTV, and I would eat out every night!" She turns to me, her cheeks red from the cold. "No worries." She winks. "I'd make sure to take care of you."

"Thanks, Fisher," I say.

We have the entire wall, but we still sit smushed together. We couldn't get any closer if we tried. Every so often one of us takes a long deep breath, we giggle, we promise to write. Then Fisher, who has already given me more than I could ever give her, digs into her bag and pulls out a carefully wrapped gift.

I'm speechless.

I have tears in my eyes, but it's too cold to cry.

"Oh, just rip it!" she tells me, as I attempt to undo the tape with my frozen fingers. Inside the box, wrapped in tissue paper is a beautiful hand-knit sweater. Ruby red.

"Fisher," I gasp. It's just about the prettiest thing I have ever seen.

I shake my head. "It's so pretty."

"Maybe you should become a fashion designer, or—"

"Do you like it?" she asks. "Really, because if you don't, um, I could like, um, knit you a—"

"It's gorgeous." To prove my point, even though it's about ten billion degrees below zero and the wind is blustery and cold, I take my parka off, slide off the sweater I have on, and slip the red knit wool over my head.

"You're going to catch pneumonia!" Fisher tells me, but I can tell by her eyes she doesn't mind my admiration, my astonishment, my complete and utter amazement at her skill, her over-the-top generosity, the fact that she made me such an exquisite thing.

I feel around in my parka's pocket. "I brought something along for the occasion," I say, my teeth kind of chattering.

"Oh, no!" Fisher teases. "Please tell me you aren't drinking again!"

I laugh. "You know I won't be doing that anytime soon!"

I pull out Ava's cell phone.

She let me borrow it for the afternoon.

"A cell phone?" Fisher is confused. "No offense, but those things don't work around here, so if that's my Christmas present, ahh—" She laughs.

"Um, no," I say, shivering. "You'll be getting that in a few days, in the mail."

"Really?" Fisher sounds intrigued.

"This is Ava's satellite phone." I fumble with it. "It has, like—" The buttons are minuscule, my fingers are frozen solid. I blow on my hands and rub them together.

"Oh, does it have one of those cameras?" asks Fisher, her face lighting up. "That's so slick," she says, watching me over my shoulder. "There. See it?" she says, looking on. "Press CAMERA."

"How'd you know that?" I ask.

"Just another one of my gifts." Fisher shrugs.

"Wait." She jumps up, reaches down, and pulls me to my feet. "Let's turn around so the mountains are in the background."

"Good thinking!" I say.

Fisher and I stand on the old stone wall, nothing but sky and mountains behind us, arms draped around each other.

I hold the little phone open in front of us, and the two of us lean together, cheek to frozen cheek. Best friends.

"Say cheese!" I say.

"CHEESE!" we say together, smiling.

"Oh, take one of me," I say. "And then I'll take one of you." I take off my hat and ruffle out my hair. I smile big and wide, and look back into Fisher's eyes. I take one of her too, slip the phone back in my pocket, and jump down onto the frozen ground.

"Em?"

"Fisher?"

"I wish I could come with you," she says softly.

"I wish you could too," I answer.

I wish you could too.

back home.

The first thing I do when I get back to the cabin is fire up the hot tub, strip off every article of clothing, and thaw my frozen body under the stars. I soak until I am boiled, bubbling, cooked like a stew. In the bathroom I slather on the lavender oil and some arnica I find by the sink. I spring up to the loft, slip on some warm jeans, Fisher's beautiful red wool sweater, dry socks, and dump out the contents of my backpack onto the top of my bed. I sort through the crumpled-up homework, the pens, the

226

mangled wrapped tampons, until I find what I'm looking for.

The article.

About me.

I sit down on the floor, my back leaning up against
the bed, and take out Ava's satellite phone.

I don't exactly entirely know what I'm doing.

I hope this works.

I have to squint to read the tiny little letters
printed on the numbers key, but finally I punch in the
text message.

To: JTW@personalitiesmag.com
Re: Grace Kincaid.

Exclusive photo.
Send payment to:
Fisher Rae
General Delivery
Medicine Hat, AK

Then I scroll through the photos. Adorable.

I look happy.

Happier than I've ever been.

I press **ATTACH PHOTO**.

Then **SEND**.

two minutes later.

After I did what I just did.

I am startled by Ava's voice.

"Emily!" she calls, which makes me laugh, because usually she does not address me in this manner in the comforts of home—

I look over my railing.

Teague.

TEAGUE!

"Hey!" I say, my face exploding with light and love as I slide down the ladder.

"Hey," he says, smiling back. Without hesitation he wraps his arms around me.

And I melt.

I melt into him.

rumor.

We hug for forever.

The longest hug of my life.

I don't even care that Ava and T are looking on from the couch. I just like, collapse into his arms.

"There's a rumor going around," he whispers.

My heart sinks.

I let go.

I look into his eyes.

"There is?"

"Yeah, I talked to Fisher, and she said—"

Oh! Fisher! Phew!

"You're heading out." Teague looks sad.

I look sad.

I am sad.

Teague looks at Ava and back at me.

"If it's okay with Ava—" He pauses and loops his fingers around mine. "I would love the pleasure of your company for one last night."

We both turn toward Ava like two love-starved teenagers.

Wait, we are love-starved teenagers!

"Ava?" I ask in my sweetest pretty-please voice.

She rolls her eyes and rests her head on T's shoulder.

"Do you think I'm the Grinch who stole Christmas? Of course you can go!"

"I can?"

"You can," she says, amused by my excitement.

There is a lot of love in this room.

A lot of love.

Teague's not done.

"Um." He looks at Ava. "If Emily would like to, and

it's okay with you—" He squeezes my hand. "I was thinking we could stay out at my cabin."

My eyes pop out of my head.

My jaw drops.

My eyebrows arch.

"Say what!" T looks up from his book.

But Ava turns to him and says something in his ear. Then, in what can only be explained as a true Christmas miracle, she looks back at me.

"Okay," she says, gleaming back at us.

"It's okay with me."

winter wonderland.

We snowshoe to the river. Take gorgeous and times it by ten. The trees in the forest are heavy, their limbs sagging, the brilliant white snow glimmering by the reflection of the moon. I think I'm walking in a dream.

What I didn't know is how close Ava's cabin is to the dollhouse. There is a shortcut up the back of the hill, along the side ridge of trees. And before I know it, Teague and I are on the shore of the rumbling, spitting, ice-cold, mostly frozen river.

My heart is shivering. "Please tell me we don't have to cross this thing."

Teague smiles. "You'll see."

We snowshoe a ways up the shore of the river, until he stops, takes off his pack, and sets it down on the ice.

"We could probably get across by foot," he tells me as he effortlessly climbs up a tree. "But this is more fun."

He pulls down a handle attached to a pulley thingamajig, and I suddenly realize we are going to be flying across the river, like circus performers on a trapeze.

I'm going first.

Teague straps me in, attaching the pulley to a cable suspended across the water.

He checks and rechecks all the cords, making sure they are snug. "You're set!" he says, smiling at me.

I shimmy up the tree and, holding the trapeze bar tight, leap out over the crackling glacial ice.

On the other side I scream with exhilaration.

My voice echoes across the forest, waking, I'm sure, every moose within miles. I can't stop smiling as I unhook myself and hurl the bar as hard as I can back over the wire toward Teague. He makes fast work, joining me in a matter of minutes. He is quiet in his confidence. His hands are warm, and I hold one as the two of us walk together up the snow-covered steps to the dollhouse cabin.

kiss.

Yes.

The second we arrive safe and sound inside the cute little cabin.

Teague Denali takes me, willingly, in his arms.

He doesn't make a big production of it. He doesn't give me time to be nervous.

He just looks into my eyes.

"Emily," he says.

"Teague." I giggle nervously.

His lips are soft and easy, and when they meet mine I somehow know what to do.

fire.

We kiss for forever, until we have to like, come up for air. One, because we are both still wearing our parkas, hats, mittens, snow pants, and backpacks, so we're hot—not to mention, the love is steaming up the place.

Teague gives me some matches, and I light the beeswax candles and some lanterns while he gets the woodstove fired up. I take the blanket off the chair and spread it out in front of the fire.

"Hey," he tells me, "I'll be right back."

"Where are you going?"

"Dinner." He smiles and slips out the door.

I won't lie. I'm a little nervous while he's gone.

I mean, there are bears out here, and it's quiet—really quiet—so I just sit there and tell myself that he is strong.

And sure enough, Teague slips back in, holding up not one but two trout and grinning a big fat grin. He caught them upstream, by a hot spring.

I watch as Teague sets the fish on a board and runs the knife from the eyes to the brain. He gingerly opens up the belly and pull the guts out. Next, he removes the fins, then the tail, before he finally cuts the length of the fish and slices out two fleshy fillets. He wraps them in foil and leaves them both on top of the stove. The alder wood is gray and burning red.

We say a blessing for the fish before we eat. Teague is special like that. Very spiritual. Sweet. After dinner we lie back on the blanket on the floor. We talk about a million things, like how we met, and what he was thinking, and what I was thinking when we first saw each other. I tell him I thought I was dreaming when I opened my eyes in the muddy ditch and saw his dimples and his beautiful eyes.

Our faces are like two inches apart, the candles have

burned out and just the light of the fire emits an orange glow.

"I wish you could stay," he says softly.

"Yeah," I say, and wonder when we are going to get back to kissing. I like kissing.

I really like kissing.

"I want to thank you for something," says Teague. "Ever since you came to Medicine Hat, Ava's been herself again—"

Huh?

"When everything happened—" Teague pauses.

"Um, what do you mean?"

"With my dad." Teague looks surprised. "Didn't Ava tell you?"

"Tell me what?"

"My dad and Ava were, well, they were together, for years. That's why she moved out here. They owned a guide company together, before Ava got sick."

I look confused.

I am confused.

"You know, the breast cancer."

Of course. That's how she knows my mom. I can't believe I never even asked. I feel like—

Oh my God.

Teague, of course, thinks I know all this. He smiles like he's remembering. "They were pretty crazy together.

My dad was the best river guide, and he was a bush pilot too. They were like, wow, they were awesome together. They were—" He pauses. "They were a team."

I've never heard Teague talk this much.

"Right before my dad died, they bought this land together. That's how—"

"Wait," I interrupt. "You share the land with Ava?"

Teague smiles. "You didn't know any of this, did you?"

"Not exactly," I answer.

"Well." Teague sits up, then stands, offering me his hand. "Sorry to drop it all on you tonight, but—"

"That's okay." I stand too.

"Here, I want to show you something." He gestures toward the door. "You just need your boots."

I slip them on in the darkness.

We walk out onto the porch, in the bright moon-light.

I have to squint until my eyes adjust.

The snow is fantastic.

I've never seen so much.

Teague kneels down on the ice-encrusted porch and brushes off something in the corner.

It's square.

A bronze plaque.

The letters are raised, embossed.

IN MEMORY OF

TEAGUE DENALI

FATHER, SON, FRIEND

GREATER LOVE HATH

NO MAN THAN THIS,

THAT A MAN LAY DOWN HIS LIFE

FOR ANOTHER

"He drowned," says Teague.

"Drowned?"

"Yeah."

"Who did he save?" I ask.

"My brother."

back inside.

We get the fire roaring, and lie down with the blanket covering us.

Teague holds me.

I cry.

I don't really truly know why.

Teague kisses my tears. "You are beautiful," he whispers. "You know that, right?"

I smile and kiss him back.

"Thank you," I say, in between kisses.

I'm not sure what to say.

But I surprise myself.

"Could you tell me again?" I whisper.

"You, are, beautiful," he speaks softly, and kisses me.

The longest sweetest kiss.

He wraps his arms around me and hugs me tight.

"We fit," I say.

"I know," he whispers, and kisses my neck.

A thousand tingling shivers go down my back.

"Where did you get these muscles?" he says softly, sweetly, as he kisses my shoulders, then back up my neck, and finds my lips again.

I want to tell him.

But he'll know.

He'll know soon enough.

forever.

We just kiss. To me, that's enough right now. Teague is sleeping, in his jeans. Okay, if you must know, he takes off his shirt. *I know*. But that's it, all clothing remains on, and he sleeps like a prince, curled up next to me, his arm a pillow placed under my head. I lie awake and think of a billion things. The way my lips feel—

Kind of raw, kind of puffy. It's like, all this time I didn't even know they were there. And now, I can feel them. *I can feel*. I keep running my tongue over them, again and again, just to make sure I'm not dreaming.

I glance out the window into the night.

This rugged grateful dreamy place.

"Merry Christmas," I whisper, mostly to me.

I close my eyes, drink in the darkness.

I'm not scared anymore.

I can see.

exodus.

Ava and I drive down the driveway one last time, in the darkness. The bumps are familiar. I know where each one is, each gaping hole, each dip. We pass the place where we got stuck that first night, then the place I met Teague, the Lookout. For most of the ride, neither of us speaks. It's too sad, too hard. But when we pass by Main Street, almost to the harbor, where we're going to meet T at the floatplane, I say something. I have to.

"Ava," I start. "Teague told me, about the—"

"His dad?" She smiles quietly. "Or the cancer."

"Both," I say.

She sighs and pulls into the empty, barely plowed lot by the harbor.

The last time we were here was in September.

Now everything has changed.

It's different.

My life has gone from meaningless to meaningful,

and it's thanks to Ava, and to this beautiful place.

Ava turns off the truck.

We climb out.

We walk together across the snowy lot, toward T, on the dock, the drumming dock, where the floatplane is waiting.

I hug Ava.

And I notice.

I notice then.

Ava Grady, the strongest woman I know, is crying. Soft, wet tears. This time I'm the one to comfort her.

"I'm so glad you're okay," I whisper.

"I'm so thankful," I say.

seattle.

When T and I step off the plane in Seattle, there are at least forty photographers snapping pictures, lights flashing in my face.

T instinctively steps in front of me.

"Easy," he says, falling into his natural role.

"Ace," they yell.

"Ace, over here."

"Hey, Ace! Ace!"

But I stride right in front of T.

"Take it easy, guys," I demand.

"Show's over, folks," I say, with a wink.

My voice is clear and strong.

"From now on," I say, smiling. "Please, call me Grace."

part six

"The world cannot be discovered by a journey of miles . . .

but only by a spiritual journey, a journey of one inch,

very arduous and humbling and joyful,

by which we arrive with the ground at our feet,

and learn to be at home."

—Wendell Berry

boxing day.

The day after Christmas, the photo, an exclusive taken by a newcomer nobody had heard of named Fisher Rae, appears on the cover of *Personalities* magazine. The picture they used was of me standing on the wall, the mountains in the background. By publishing it before everyone else, *Personalities* makes the photos of me at the airport worthless. *Personalities* magazine already had me in my sealskin parka. They had the scoop. And Fisher doesn't even know it yet, but she will be getting a check—a big check—bigger than she can possibly imagine, in the mail in a few days. Ava is going to set up a trust fund for her so she doesn't spend it all in one place.

Thanks to satellite TV, by the day after Christmas,

everyone on the island knows who I am. And of course, the paparazzi came. They came in droves. After the storm. They stood out like a sore thumb in their bright yellow snowsuits. One guy even offered Abe twenty bucks for any stories he could tell. To my great surprise, Abe told the guy to—

Well, you can guess what Abe told him, it's two words he uses a lot. Not one person talked. Medicine Hat looked out for me, protected me like a native, a daughter, one of them. Their lips, mum. Plus, it's winter still. The days are hard and cold and short, though getting longer. There is no time for *Entertainment Tonight*, or *Inside Edition*. There's wood to chop, fish to harvest.

Life to live.

Real life.

Teague got his Christmas present too. As we speak, a truck should be pulling up on Main Street, and the deliveryman will open the old red door, hike up the narrow stairway next to Sadie's, and ask Boy Wonder where he would like it.

His brand-new snowmobile.

Lest you think that's too materialistic, I also knitted him my very first sweater. It's blue.

I sewed in my own little tag, it says—

MADE BY GRACE.

Ava sent her Christmas present to me with T. It was

hard to get through security. Beverly, my trusty ax, mounted to a wooden board with an inscription—

LONG LIVE BEVERLY!

COME BACK SOON.

LOVE, A.G.

MEDICINE HAT, AK

later.

In Malibu, I purge almost everything.

Get down to the basics.

My room, my clothes. I use Ava's rule: anything I haven't worn, used, or thought of in a year, I give away to someone who could use it. Not just charity—friends too. People who are close to me.

Including my money.

As per my instructions, just as we had planned, by the time I got back, Mariko had distributed all of it, every last cent. Including a significant anonymous contribution to one Theona Briggs, to be used for the Island of Medicine Hat and the community health services, at her discretion.

I'll make more.

I was hitting yesterday, just in the back of my house, against the wall, by the beach. After three months in

Alaska, not doing one single sit-up, I've got my groove back.

I love it.

Tennis, I mean.

Besides my mom and Mariko, nobody knows this yet, but I am going to play again. This time, on my own terms.

EPSN and *Sports Illustrated*, sure, they come with the territory. I am happy to speak with a sports reporter about my game.

But no more modeling.

No cosmetic lines.

Or skimpy little outfits.

No more interviews, photo shoots, magazine covers.

And no more staff or publicists.

If I have something to say.

I'll say it—myself.

Thanks to a certain Surf Goddess, I try to speak obligingly, clearly, with a smile.

Oh, and this summer—

Glad you asked.

I'm spending this summer with friends.

My best friends. In this magical place where in the summer the sun never sets. Where the daylight, at its peak, is eighteen hours long.

This time I'm going as me, Grace.

No more lies.

My hair is honey blond and long. I can pull it back again.

Still have the ruby in my nose.

My mom's coming too. Me, Mariko, Fisher, we're going on a guided trip. My treat. We're staying with Tobias and Ava—in *their* cabin, or maybe out back. We're going to kayak near the fjords, by glaciers and whales, climb mountains, go rafting down Eagle River.

Our guide?

Dark eyes.

Dimples.

Sweet, kissable lips.

Yes.

Right.

A Note from the Author

I am most grateful to my editor, Brenda Bowen, whose grace and skill guides this story; and to my agent at ICM, Richard Abate, whose savvy insight is my good fortune.

Special thanks also to Hyperion/Disney Publishing Worldwide—a truly talented group of people; and to International Creative Management, expressly Kate Lee, James Gregorio, and Margaret Marr.

To the sweethearts in my hometown and beyond whose kindness lifts, lightens, shines—*Thank you.*